THE HAUNTING OF GRANT MANSION

MARIE WILKENS

❀ Created with Vellum

THE MANSION

Scratching. Always scratching. The noise carried through the estate night and day. To the untrained ear, one might think the expected mice that took shelter there had finally overthrown the manor's human occupants. Yet it never ceased, and even rodents needed their rest. Some would wonder, upon hearing it for days, if there were spirits shuffling their feet somewhere in the attic above them. Even on the sunniest of afternoons, when every ancient window and door was opened, you could find the faint noise reminiscent of a fingernail being dragged across a bone. It had become something of a mystery in the tightly knit community.

A few locals had even gone so far as asking old Benjamin Grant himself what it was. He'd look at them like they'd lost their minds before announcing there was no such sound. No one had ever pressed him further than that. In part, the locals knew it was a moot point. He'd been slowly losing his mind for some time. There was a darker side to their silence, though, a kinship built on greed. Grant Manor sat at the edge of Willowbrook, a town growing in tourism, thanks to its lakefront location. The pristine body of water was aptly named for its location. Grant Lake was privately owned, though the city had tried for years to take possession of it.

At every litigation, Benjamin would represent himself and come out on top, fervently taking notes with his antique inkwell and quill. Some wondered how a man in his state could gain custody of his wards, but others assumed, rightfully, that he'd bought his way through the system to become their legal guardian. Still, those closest to him were vehemently loyal. His staff adored him and the twins alike. They'd often be seen walking the grounds and fishing from the dock. It was impossible not to notice the love in the old man's eyes when he was with them.

He was reminiscent of the man the townsfolks had known before the accident. Benjamin didn't think about that night anymore. As a matter of fact, he didn't think about anything except the manor and the twins. In earnest, he didn't have time to think about the scratching. It was the least of his problems. There was something after him, after the children. Everyone said their mother's death had been tragic but unavoidable. Benjamin knew better. The house had claimed her, just as it was trying to do to him.

Maria had been his loyal house manager for ten years. Her son and daughter had been born on the property four years after she had started her career with him. Their father had quickly shown himself to be nothing more than a deadbeat passing through, but Benjamin regarded Maria as his own daughter. Instantly, he made sure she was well provided for. When the twins came along, they brought with them a life and warmth that Grant Manor hadn't seen since Benjamin's son had run the halls decades prior.

The house will give you everything, then rip it away. It will destroy your mind. Even now, it torments me with images of my death. Last night, I was certain I felt a noose being placed around my neck while I slept alone in a locked room.

Benjamin's hand moved with surprising speed for his age as the quill moved across the pages of his journal.

Every night, I hear it moving against me, waiting to claim another one of us. The children, thank God, don't hear it. It's not after them, at least not yet.

Behind him, a warm breath caught the nape of his neck. He squeezed his eyes closed as his hand trembled. After months of torment, Benjamin knew better than to turn around despite his instinct to do so. The empty darkness haunted the recesses of his mind. A cool sensation moved up his arm to the back of his head, pressing at his skull. Would a knife be the house's torture that night? He shuddered and dipped his quill into the well, fervently writing down every memory before it was stolen from him. It didn't matter that he was retired from his career as an author. The crippling arthritis in his hands was a reminder of his success. Pushing through the pain, he started to write again. He had to warn them.

Stay away from the water after sunset. That's how they got my Maria.

The study door flew open. Vera and Marcus bounded in with no regard for their caretaker's ailing body as they scrambled onto his lap for a final embrace before bedtime. Benjamin held them close. There was no telling when he'd succumb to the house and the evil that sought out those who held its deed. Just seconds after the twins left him again, the sensation of not being alone returned. He turned his attention back to the journal.

I've taken one final step to protect them. One last measure to keep them safe, but at what cost? I've condemned another in their place. God, help my soul.

The blade pressed against his neck. In the split second before it pierced through his frail skin, Benjamin cried out in horror. A familiar hand wrapped around his lips and nose. As it dawned on him what was happening, he felt the blade puncture his skin. Within a minute, the last heir to the Grant fortune was dispatched. The man pulled his knife out of Benjamin's lifeless body, a trail of blood following after him as he moved silently through the house.

The aged floorboards creaked outside the children's bedroom. Their giggles could be heard on the other side as they whispered before bedtime. Vera saw him enter the room though Marcus continued to keep his back turned, singing a bedtime song with childhood gusto. A progression of excitement, then confusion, and finally fear played across Vera's features as her eyes moved down to the bloodied knife in the intruder's hand. A scream pierced the night, followed by a silence the estate hadn't known in decades.

The scratching of Benjamin's quill no longer filled the halls of Grant Manor.

"It's only when you can see through the darkness that you'll truly realize your full potential. By taking the first step to better your future, you can see growth in the next year. With our online course—"

Mike fished the phone from his pocket, quickly skipping to the start of the next podcast as he shoved the worn postbox key into its home. He grabbed the contents, quickly flipping through them. The first three were bills, all with the same yellow and red "final notice" warning printed on the outside. A year prior, it would have sent a flush of embarrassment coursing through Mike. It had been so long since they'd paid anything on time, though, that the sinking sensation of failure no longer caused his stomach to curl into knots.

It didn't matter anyway. Mike's hand froze when he came across the next envelope. He'd already started up the narrow steps to the small apartment he shared with his wife and daughter. Shoving the rest of the mail into his computer bag, Mike ripped into the letter, jerking the document from its sheath with trembling hands. The eruption of joy was short-lived as his eyes moved across the page.

Dear Mr. Grant,

We regret to inform you that we will be passing on your manuscript, A Culprit in Canterbury. *While we found your writing style unique, the characters lacked true depth and emotion.*

"Son of a bitch," Mike whispered.

He crumpled the letter in his hand, quickly scurrying up the remaining four flights to the seventh story. The apartment door stuck as he shoved his shoulder into it. They'd lived in the same run-down building for five years, and never once had he seen an improvement made to the property. Still, it was all they could afford, thanks to him. Guilt coursed through Mike as he dropped the mail onto the table with his bag. The letter stayed balled in his hand, the edges of the paper digging into his palm as he stormed to the small bedroom that doubled as his home office.

Soon, Callie would be home, and he'd have to break the news to her. How anyone could love a failed writer like Mike was something he struggled to understand. Most nights, when he couldn't sleep, he'd ask himself if she only stayed for the sake of Elizabeth. The anxiety of losing them both would keep him up until the wee hours of the morning. The voices in his head always knew where to strike. Whenever Mike's depression started to take hold of him, Callie would reassure him that their love was pure and true. How much that voice of reason really helped, though, neither of them could be certain.

Collapsing into his worn chair, he tossed the letter onto the desk and glared at it. Its presence there mocked him. The laptop that usually took its spot was still in the bag. Behind him, across from the secondhand bed, the clock's hands ticked by slowly, without Mike moving from the chair. His eyes stayed trained on the letter as the tension inside of him continued to build, the guilt starting to simmer. A rustling in the hall caught his attention seconds before the front door opened again. He quickly darted out of the bedroom just in time to see the pair walk in.

"Is everything okay?" he asked.

Clarissa sighed as she shrugged off her raincoat before taking Lizzy's. The little girl darted away from the pair before curling up on the threadbare sofa.

"I tried to call you from the hospital. Lizzy got sick at school," Clarissa said. "The phones got shut off again, didn't they?"

Mike grabbed his cell. "Shit. I'm sorry, sweetheart. I meant to call them this afternoon to get an extension."

"It's okay; I get paid Friday. We'll get them back on then. I had to leave work early, though. Mark wasn't happy."

"Mark can go fu—"

"Mike! Stop it!" Clarissa hissed. "He's my supervisor, and this is the second time this month I've had to leave early. I can't blame him for being upset."

"Of course not; Mark could never do anything wrong,"

Mike growled.

Clarissa's jaw dropped. "Hey, where is this coming from? If it's the phones, don't worry about it, sweetheart. We'll be okay. Plus, your book will get published soon. Then we can look back on this and laugh."

Mike cringed as he quickly turned away from his concerned wife. She was going to be so disappointed in him, again. Another failure. Maybe this time, it would be the one to drive her into the arms of her bastard boss. Had it not been for the benefits and pay, he'd insist on her finding another place to work as a nurse. He had to keep it together for her. She couldn't know about the rejection, not yet. There was still a chance one of the other publishers would pick up his work.

"You're right. I'm sorry. Things have just been rough lately. I hate that you have to work so many hours. I've been thinking about getting a job down at the coffee shop. God knows I'm there enough."

"We've talked about this. I can cover the bills…well, almost. You're down there for the Wi-Fi, not to work for minimum wage. You keep trying to find something as a freelancer, okay?"

"How did I get so lucky?" Mike asked. "You've got to be an angel."

Clarissa smiled as she went to her husband, taking his hand in hers as she kissed Mike's cheek lovingly. Despite everything they were going through, the spark between them had never died. He turned to her, the tension now fading from his eyes as he kissed Clarissa's forehead before pulling her into his arms the rest of the way.

"Don't worry, honey. This too shall pass, okay? I'm going to make Lizzy some soup. Are you working?"

"I was just getting ready to. Why don't you let me take care of Lizzy? You look beat. Go grab a shower."

"You don't have to tell me twice," Clarissa said.

She gave Mike one final kiss before slipping into the bedroom. Mike grabbed a pot and a can of soup from the cupboard. The old gas stove flickered to life just as he dumped the can's contents into the tiny pot, stirring as he listened to the cartoons Lizzy had started watching in the next room. His mind was starting to focus again. Clarissa's positivity was like a drug to him. While the soup cooked, Mike grabbed the rest of the mail and started to open it, slowly making mental notes of who he still needed to call. Anxiety clutched his heart when he saw the legal heading of the last letter. The only time attorneys contacted people was when the debt collectors failed.

"Why didn't you tell me?"

Mike jumped and spun around to see Clarissa. She was wrapped in a towel and holding the crumpled rejection letter. Heat jumped to his cheeks. He couldn't meet her eyes. The sadness in them was too much. Tearing open the envelope, he tried to distract himself as he pretended to read.

"I didn't want you looking at me like that," Mike mumbled.

"Mike, we are supposed to be a team…."

At the top of the letter, a name caught his attention. It was one he'd only heard in passing from his father and never with any emotion other than anger and contention.

"Are you listening to me?" Clarissa asked.

"What?" Mike asked, his head jerking up. "No, I'm sorry. It's this letter."

"What's going on?"

"I don't know," Mike stammered. "This guy says he's an attorney, and I've been named as the benefactor in a will."

She frowned. "That doesn't make any sense. Your father's been dead for years."

"It's not my father. It's my grandfather," he said. "Well, it *was* my grandfather."

Clarissa gasped. "I thought you said you didn't know him. Your father never talked about him at all before he passed away. Are you sure it's not a scam?"

"I didn't know him," he muttered. "It doesn't look like I'm going to get the chance, either. He died in a murder-suicide a few months ago. I don't know how it could be a scam. This lawyer said he's been looking for me for weeks."

"Holy cow. The lawyer said he left you something? I sure hope it's not big. Otherwise, it will never fit in this place."

"Honey, he left me his house...or should I say, his estate. We have to call this guy, and then we can go look at it. I've never heard of the place before. I wonder if the market is any good. We could probably sell it. He said it's about six hours from here."

"Oh my God," Clarissa whispered. "Mike, do you know what this means?"

Mike grinned. "Yeah, we don't have to worry about bills anymore."

2

"*I* just don't get why we had to come down here for the reading," Callie whispered. "We could have done this over the phone."

Mike wrapped his arm around his wife, kissing her forehead as Lizzy played on the floor in front of them. The small office was packed with comfy oddities. It didn't have the traditionally cold feel of an attorney's office. Granted, the aging attorney didn't get much traffic from what the duo had gathered on the drive into the small town. Despite the lack of activity, the pair had been waiting almost an hour. They'd made it to the town of Belington hours after their initial appointment time.

"I don't know, but I'm sure we will find out soon enough," Mike offered.

Callie groaned. "Really? I'm starting to wonder if this old fart is going to come in today at all."

"The receptionist said he just stepped out for lunch. Don't forget, we were the ones who were late."

"Yeah, but we called him four hours ago when our car broke down. Lizzy is getting hungry. I don't know how much longer we're going to be able to wait."

"Why don't the two of you run across the road to that diner and get something to eat?"

Callie frowned. A dinner out wasn't in the budget. There was plenty of food in the cooler they'd left in the car. The strange little town had almost no parking, with the only free spaces being nearly seven blocks from their destination. After spending several hundred dollars of their rent money on a mechanic, the idea of another expense sent Callie's stomach into knots. She'd missed another shift at the hospital to make the journey with Mike. If his grandfather's estate didn't pay out a handsome sum, they'd be evicted for certain.

"Everything is going to be fine," Mike whispered. "Stop worrying about money, sweetheart. This is the break we've been waiting for. Go get yourselves something to eat."

"I can just walk to the car—"

"Callie," Mike was stern, "take Lizzy to the diner before you have a panic attack about money."

"Mike, I really don't think—"

The receptionist cleared her throat. Callie's cheeks flushed as she realized the woman must have heard the entire conversation. Both parents looked in her direction as she nodded her head toward a small fridge and display of snacks they hadn't noticed in the corner before. Callie smiled at her in unspoken appreciation. She rose and made her way to the corner to look over the selection. Grabbing a bag of apple slices and a cheese stick for Lizzy, Callie returned to her seat next to Mike and offered her daughter the treats. Immediately, the girl started in on them, and a fleeting moment of content silence filled the small space.

Just as Lizzy popped the last apple slice into her mouth, the front door opened, and the graying man from the painting above them appeared. He seemed shocked to find clients waiting for him. The woman behind the desk scurried out to meet him. She quickly took his briefcase as he shuffled over to the trio, who were now captivated by his presence. Lizzy knew nothing about what was going on except that they'd had a wonderful day, pack to the brim with adventures and new places. Even at her young age, she'd picked up on her parents' change in demeanor. There was a tense excitement in the air.

"You've got his nose," the man grumbled. "Well, let's get this show on the road."

Without another word, he walked slowly through the only other door in the building. The couple followed after him, cramming into the two chairs opposite the attorney's desk, flanked by towers of boxes. Callie grabbed Lizzy and held her tightly in her lap, terrified one of the looming skyscrapers would come tumbling down on the curious little girl. Lizzy always managed to find herself in the most obscure of situations. Calling the child inquisitive seemed to be a drastic understatement for the exhausted parents. Neither moved as they waited for their host to position himself behind the desk.

"So, you're old Ben's grandson then? I must say, I'm

damn shocked to see you here," he said. "The man seemed well enough when I last saw him. Guess the mind can go south at any point, though."

"You knew my grandfather?" Mike asked.

"Course I did! Hell, me and old Benny boy went to school together. That was a hot minute ago, though. I never thought the last time he changed his will would be our last coffee and catch up."

"He changed it three months ago? Do you know why? I'm sorry...I just never knew him."

"Well now, that's a family matter I couldn't speak to. I know he went through a good bit of trouble to find you, though. Always seemed odd to me that he didn't want to reach out to you. I reckon that's not my place to have an opinion on, either. I suppose we should just get right down to it."

"And what exactly is *it*, if you don't mind my asking?" Callie said.

"About five million dollars in assets," he grumbled. "Now, that's not the value of the manor itself. Let me look here at the fine print. Always something in the fine print...lousy old fart that man was."

Callie gasped as Mike started to cough. The tickle in his throat had come with a fury after hearing the dollar amount. It would be more than enough to keep them afloat. Yet the old man was still shuffling through the pages of the will, unfazed by the couple's obvious reactions of shock. It was a life-altering moment, yet the attorney could have been sitting alone for all he knew.

"Of that, a little over half is accounted for in the estate itself—"

"Estate? Like a house?" Mike asked.

The man glared at him. "You want me to finish or start asking questions? Because we can't do both at the same time, and this would go a lot faster if you held your tongue."

His harsh reaction caught Callie off guard. While she hid her emotions well, beneath it, she could sense a level of hostility from the self-proclaimed classmate of Mike's grandfather. Pursing her lips, Callie bit her tongue to keep herself from saying something she might later regret. It wouldn't do to make an enemy of the man holding their fortune and future in his hands.

"Now, where was I...yes, the estate. The property itself is worth a good bit of money. There are artifacts, collectibles, and other trinkets you could sell, I'm sure," he looked at Mike with disdain.

Callie was now positive she was picking up on anger. Neither of them spoke as he paused. Like scolded children, they waited silently for him to continue.

"Benjamin was adamant that any cash holdings, stocks, and bonds of miscellaneous value go to a list of charities he left with me. However, the estate, that is, Grant Manor and its contents have been bequeathed to you, Mr. Grant."

After a lengthy silence that assured the man was done, Mike spoke in disbelief. "This manor, it was left to me?"

"That's what I said, isn't it? He'd intended for everything to go to Vera and Marcus...but that changed, it seems. He changed if you believe the rumors, of course."

"Rumors?" Callie asked.

"This estate, it's worth millions?" Mike asked.

"Are you hard of hearing or something?"

"No," Mike said with a chuckle. "You have to understand, though, I never met my grandfather. He and my father weren't close. I just don't know why a complete stranger would leave me his house—"

"Manor," the man grumbled. "Show it some respect. It's a local landmark, not some run-down shanty on the edge of town."

"I apologize," Mike muttered. "This is all just really shocking for us. So what's the next step? Do we get appraisers out there? How fast can we get it on the market?"

"You don't want to see it?"

"No," Mike said.

"Mike," Callie hissed.

"What? It's not like we want to live down here, right? I don't see any point. As he's pointed out, it's not a little shanty; it's a freaking manor. What are we going to do with a *manor*?"

"Still, we should go see it, if nothing else than to pay our respects," Callie said.

"What you do with it, I don't care. However, I wouldn't go seeing dollar signs just yet," the attorney growled. "Your grandfather made it clear in the will that you cannot sell Grant Manor under any circumstances."

"What?" Callie stammered.

Mike's face paled, his jaw dropping in shock. Apart from the fact that the property was a manor, it was hours from their home. They had no use for a manor or a life in the obviously hostile town. They sat in stunned silence, each processing the plethora of information that had come tumbling down on their shoulders. For Mike, the potential ran rampant. His artistic mind was already filling the unseen estate with art and guests alike.

Dread filled Callie. She could see the wheels spinning behind Mike's eyes. The idea that he was searching for an escape from his writing had plagued her before. Now it seemed the distraction might take root for the first time. How much more their strained marriage could take, though, she couldn't be sure. It seemed his heritage was playing a sick joke on them. Callie suddenly found herself being dragged by her excited husband the seven blocks back to their car. Unfortunately, they were no longer going home.

3

"I can't believe we're doing this," Callie growled.

Mike smiled at her, patting her leg as they followed the navigation on his phone to Grant Manor. Her trepidations were warranted. After being told the estate still had electricity and water, he'd all but begged his wife on bended knee to stay there for the evening. Callie had never been able to tell Mike no, though he rarely used the ability. Despite the rough patches in their relationship, the duo made a point of working through things. Neither wanted Lizzy to grow up in a broken home.

"Come on, sweetheart. Think of it like an adventure. Plus, we are saving money on a hotel for the night."

"I don't know that we would have done that, either. I still think we should go straight home. He said it has six bedrooms, each with an accompanying bathroom. That's way too much space for us!"

"We could rent out some of the rooms, you know. The

attorney said Ben had lived in it, so it won't be run-down. Look, we're here."

Callie stared out at the sprawling estate as they turned onto the winding driveway. Lined on either side by ancient oak trees, the lane never seemed to end. Beyond the house, you could make out the lake in the distance with a dock and boathouse bobbing gently on the water. Grant Manor towered over their little sedan as they came to a halt at its grand entrance. Despite being surrounded by nature, silence greeted the family as they climbed out of the car.

It was truly breathtaking to behold. The property was kept in pristine condition. Mike bounded up the front steps with Lizzy close behind. Callie hung back, taking in everything before following after the pair. While her husband saw the property's vast potential, Callie could see the problems. The landscaping alone would cost a small fortune. If they somehow managed to make the manor into a bed and breakfast, they would need an army of staff to maintain it.

So far, she hadn't seen another living soul since they'd left town earlier. Brushing aside her unease, Callie slowly made her way into the entrance. Despite telling herself that the silence was the only thing making the manor eerie, she still couldn't shake the unnatural sensation of being watched. Surely if anyone were in the area, they'd have approached her outside. Yet, the only noise or indication of life anywhere near her came from Mike and Lizzy as they explored. The old house creaked beneath her feet as she took in the grand parlor.

Like stepping back in time, Callie could almost feel the history of the house. Somewhere above her, she heard running steps and a little girl's laughter. It warmed her heart to know Lizzy was having the time of her life. She ran her fingers along the hand-hewn woodwork, snaking her way into the next room before coming to a sudden stop. Mike and Lizzy had found an old map of the property, now sprawled out on the floor as they rattled off the different areas.

"Wow, you two got down here fast. Is there another staircase?" she asked.

Mike shot her a queer look, shaking his head slightly before turning back to Lizzy. A chill ran down Callie's spine, her eyes darting to the lone staircase in the parlor. Taking a deep breath, she reminded herself that it had been a long day. The house was older than dirt, and sound seemed to travel differently within its hallowed halls. She listened with one ear as Mike shared his plans for turning the manor into a bed and breakfast. Yet her attention was drawn farther into the room to a painting that hung above a fireplace.

"Daddy, can I go look at the lake?" Lizzy asked.

Mike smiled and nodded.

"Mike..." Callie cautioned.

"She's been swimming since she was three, Callie," he muttered. "Plus, you won't go near the water, right?"

"Right!" the girl exclaimed.

"Fine, but I want you back here in ten minutes, got it? If I have to come looking for you—"

Lizzy was gone before her mother could finish the

hollow threat. Mike chuckled and rose, going to his wife and wrapping an arm around her waist before kissing her cheek. He'd barely stopped in his excitement to talk with her. Now he knew they had to take the brief opportunity while Lizzy was distracted to plan their future.

"So, what do you think? It's got great potential, right?" he asked.

Callie frowned. "It does if you've got six figures to sink into it. It's a lot of house for us."

"But it comes rent-free, plus, we could sell off a few of the paintings to make ends meet until business picks up."

"Business?"

Mike blushed. "Yeah, I was thinking it would be a great bed and breakfast, what with the lake right there and all. I bet we could easily be making a profit by the end of the year. Listen, there is an entire silver tea set just collecting dust in the kitchen. That money alone would get us moved and set up for a few months. We can talk to the bank down here about a loan. We have the credit rating—"

"You mean *I* have the credit," Callie snapped. "That credit is supposed to buy our first home, in the city we both love, back where I have a job that pays all our bills."

"You don't need to remind me," Mike growled.

Callie cringed; she'd struck a nerve with him. It hadn't been her intention for her to sound like she was attacking him, but he was obviously wounded by her words. She sighed and pulled him back into her arms. The tension eased from his body at once as he held her close. The strength of their love had always gotten them through the hard times. Grant Manor was shaping up to be their greatest hurdle.

"I know we're going out on a limb here. You'd be going out on one, at least. I just know this could be our big break, though."

"What about your writing?"

"I'll keep doing it. There is a beautiful study upstairs that's perfect for me. I think my grandfather must have enjoyed writing as well. It's all set up with journals and a quill."

"Do you know how hard it's going to be for me to find another job that pays what the hospital does?"

"Sweetheart, I don't want you to work at all. We'll restore this place as a family."

"I just want to make sure you understand that if we take out a loan and this goes belly-up, our entire life savings, all of our plans, my credit, everything will be gone."

"You heard what the attorney said. There are assets in the house that we can sell. I promise, if things aren't moving by the end of the year, we'll sell what we can and get out. Either way, we will still be better off financially."

"You mean that you will," Callie whispered.

"If this is about your credit, we will take a few paintings off the wall right now, and you can lock them up."

"It's not that, I'm sorry. I don't want to be Debbie Downer in all this; I'm just worried. This place gives me the creeps. Earlier, I swore I heard Lizzy upstairs."

Mike kissed his wife. "Just give it time. It's just your nerves from the drive down. Imagine what you could do with this place. You could have that garden you always wanted and time to actually cook some of the family recipes you've always talked about."

Callie knew he was going to wear her down until she agreed. It wasn't like him to be so adamant or excited about something. She had to remind herself that it was his grandfather's estate, a connection that, as a writer, he had to long for. With a dramatic sigh, she finally nodded in approval. Mike gave a shout of joy before swooping her up into his arms, showering her with kisses. Callie's temper broke as she burst into laughter, returning her husband's enthusiasm just as Lizzy came running back inside.

Despite her trepidations, Callie was determined to see the positive side of the situation. She followed Mike upstairs and explored the house with him as they found the silver set he would use to fund their move. The house was truly a museum of unique artifacts. Yet the one that stood out to her the most was a recently completed painting of Benjamin Grant and his two wards. Knowing what had happened to them gave the portrait an unnaturally eerie aura. The eyes of the children seemed to follow Callie as she passed. She shuddered and quickly followed after her family, assuring herself that it was just her imagination playing tricks again.

4

"I can't believe we are really going to live here!" Lizzy whispered.

Mike laughed. "Well, get used to it, kiddo. This is going to be our home forever."

"That sounds so ominous," Callie joked.

"What does that mean, Mommy?" Lizzy asked.

Mike grinned, cocking one brow at his wife. "Yeah, Mommy."

"Nothing, sweetheart. I'm excited we're here. Maybe we'll live here forever."

"Why would we leave, Mommy?"

"Well, maybe Daddy will sell his book and we will get to travel and see the world. Wouldn't that be fun?"

"I guess," Lizzy muttered.

"Good save, Mommy," Mike whispered.

"Well, I couldn't tell her the place gives me the willies, now, could I?" Callie hissed.

"The willies? Is that some weird religious thing I don't know about?"

"Oh, shut up," Callie said with a grin. "It's a good thing you're cute, mister."

"You know you love me."

"Uh-huh, sure," she said playfully.

Mike rolled his eyes and grinned as they pulled to a stop in front of Grant Manor for the second time. It was still hard for him to believe that just three weeks prior, he'd been struggling to keep a roof over his family's head. Now they had a few thousand dollars in the bank and were the owners of an actual estate. Callie was still struggling with the decision, but it was obvious she'd enjoyed the last few weeks at home with Lizzy. Without the stress of paying bills, Callie was positively glowing. Mike had made a point of focusing all his attention on the two women in his world, not wanting to jinx the next phase of their lives.

Before either parent could stop her, Lizzy took off once again for the lake. With the time that had passed, Callie's mind had eased about the property some. Though pulling up to it with their rented moving truck still made her stomach churn a little bit. Shoving the trepidations deep down, she followed Mike as they wandered through the house again. Mike had a smile plastered on his face, the same excitement he'd had weeks ago barely wavering with the time that had passed.

They moved with boxes up to the second floor, winding their way to the room that would be Lizzy's. It was three times the size of her old one back at the apartment. Callie eyed the two antique bedframes that sat along the wall, separated by a window overlooking the lake. From there, the pair could see Lizzy crouched down near the edge of the water, poking at the ground with a stick. There was no doubt in Callie's mind that her adventurous daughter was conversing with the two geese floating near her.

"Are you sure about this?" Callie asked, her voice low.

Mike wrapped an arm around her. "The old man went crazy. What happened was a tragedy, and those kids probably never should have been in his care. We can't let that stop us from moving forward, though."

"Yeah, but does she have to stay in this room? It's morbid."

"What do you want us to do, Callie? It's just a room, and it's the closest one to the master bedroom. Should we start shutting off parts of the house?"

"No," she mumbled. "Of course, not, but two children died in here, Mike."

"You and I know that," he hissed. "But Lizzy doesn't, and as far as I see it, she never needs to know—"

"But you heard her on the way here. She's already asking questions about them."

"We agreed to tell her there was a sad accident, nothing more. Now, the groundskeeper already took care of the mattresses and cleanup months ago, okay? If you didn't know what had happened, could you tell?"

Callie looked around, giving his question serious thought. It was one of the first things Mike had loved about her. She wasn't the type to reply off the cuff. He knew her words were carefully picked and honest. Hell, sometimes, it was her truthful encouragement and praise that kept him writing. If she saw the good in it, there had to be something. Callie sighed, leaning into Mike's chest.

"No, not at all. Heck, it doesn't even smell like cleaner in here. Just old wood and the lilies outside. I know you're right. If we cut off every room of the house that your grandfather and his kids were in, we'd be right back at the apartment."

"Everything is going to be fine, okay? Why don't I go grab the new mattress, and you can get her bed all made up? We can take apart this other frame and stick it in the attic tomorrow. Once we've got all our stuff moved in, you'll feel a lot better."

"You're right. We just need to make this place feel like a home," Callie replied, a little more confidence in her voice.

Mike kissed Callie's forehead and headed back down to the moving truck. They'd bought the new mattress on their way out of the city. He couldn't help but smile as he tugged it into the house. A month ago, the purchase would have been impossible. Half the truck contained new replacements of items they'd had for over a decade. Callie had kept them frugal, reminding Mike of the work that would need to be done on the property.

Her worry over the deaths that had taken place caused him some concern. While he'd been raised by an atheist father, Callie's family was comprised of devout Catholics. She held her own set of beliefs and superstitions, including an affection for the paranormal. Mike saw the house's morbid history as a potential selling point for business, even if he didn't believe in the same foolishness as Callie. He climbed his way up the steps to find Callie crouched down next to one of the beds.

She smiled at him, a wrench in one hand. "I thought we'd go ahead and get it out of here tonight."

"All right," he said. "Why don't you let me take over, and you go grab her bedding and stuff. She looks pretty happy out there. We could have it done in no time."

"Thank you, sweetheart. I think I'd sleep a lot easier."

"For you," Mike whispered, "anything."

He watched Callie head for the truck as he took over dismantling the bed. It quickly became apparent they hadn't been apart in several decades, if ever. The first bolt came out after three minutes of grunting and cursing. Feeling victorious, Mike moved on to the second bolt that would free one arm of the structure. He caught a glimpse of Lizzy out the window, Callie now exploring with her. The bolt gave way, sending his knuckle hard into the floor after catching the head of the bolt.

A few droplets of blood fell onto the hardwood floors as he cursed. Covering his knuckle, he bolted to his feet and jogged to the master bathroom. The faucet gave a depleted groan before dispensing a few drops of rusted water. Cursing once again, Mike snatched a towel twice his age off the rack and covered his hand. Below him, he heard Callie and Lizzy grabbing boxes from the truck. His mind raced back to the blood in the bedroom.

If his wife saw it, her mind would start playing tricks on her again. With his focus shifted, Mike quickly tied the towel around his hand while grabbing a second and racing back to the bedroom. He was too late. Mike's heart raced when he saw the duo smiling at him from the bedroom. His eyes darted to the floor. The blood was gone.

5

"*M*ike! What happened to your hand?" Callie gasped.

His eyes shifted to her but not before she caught the shocked look behind them. Callie moved quickly to her husband's side, untying the towel as Lizzy looked on with fascination.

"Oh my God, Mike, what happened? You are going to need a couple stitches. Lizzy, go grab my bag from the front seat of the truck, please. How did you do this?"

"Um, I knocked my knuckle when I was taking apart the bed. The water in the bedroom isn't working."

"What? I'm not worried about that. Come on, let's get you downstairs. The kitchen water works. We need to get this cleaned up. I'm surprised you're not bleeding more."

He followed her out of the bedroom. He was sure there was blood on the floor before. In truth, he'd never done well with blood. As a child, every big cut or scratch had made him nauseous. It didn't take long for Callie to get him stitched up. Lizzy's questioned everything her mother was doing, distracting Mike until his wife was done. Before long, they were back upstairs and finishing Lizzy's bedroom.

Within the hour, the sun was setting and the room was complete. Lizzy climbed into her new bed with heavy eyes. The bizarre incident from earlier in the afternoon was all but forgotten for Mike. He was convinced the sight of blood had messed with his mind. It was the only logical explanation. The less Callie knew about it, the better off they all would be. After settling Lizzy in her room, the pair retreated to the main parlor for a well-deserved drink in their new home.

"I'll call a plumber to take a look at this place tomorrow. I'm sure it won't be the last repairs, either. Then I'll go down to the bank and get the ball rolling on a loan."

"Okay, I'll sign whatever you need for it. I just want to get everything unpacked before we start having guests. If you worry about the house, I'll focus on everything else, like getting your office all set up."

"Perfect. Anything of my grandfather's you find, just box up, and I'll shove it into the attic tomorrow."

Callie frowned. "Are you sure? It looked like he kept a lot of journals. It might be interesting to read them. Maybe you'll find out where you got your knack for writing."

"He wasn't my grandfather. He was a stranger who ostracized my father. I don't want to have anything in common with him. He was a murderer."

"He went insane. Everyone around here seems to think

so. If he had dementia, that might be good to know as well."

"Dementia or not, he murdered two little kids. That's not something I want to be tied to. Listen, you can read them if you want, but I'd just as soon pretend like I didn't know the old coot because I didn't. Do you think people are going to want to stay with the grandchild of a serial killer?"

"All right, Mike. We'll do it however you want; I trust you."

Mike grabbed ahold of Callie's waist, pulling her into his arms as their lips met in a stolen kiss. Even after years of marriage and dating before that, the spark was still as hot as the day they'd met. Both their worries started to slip away as the moment turned into several. The stress of money and relocating was now nothing more than a distant memory. Tugging her down onto the floor, Mike was determined to remind her of their passion.

Callie relished every second of his attention, but her mind refused to stay focused on him. The house felt alive, like it was watching them. She wanted to shield her body despite there being no one but the trio within a half-dozen miles. Somewhere deep in the recesses of the house, a faint noise could be heard. Time and time again, Mike had reminded her that the ancient plumbing and wiring would surely need work. There were bound to be strange noises and little "quirks," as he called them.

He bit at her neck, driving away the last of her thoughts as she succumbed to her husband's whims. They spent a passionate hour with each other, a wanton act of lovemaking on the floor that was unlike Callie. She'd been raised with a healthy dose of Catholic guilt. Lovemaking was reserved for bedrooms and late hours, not the early evening, nude with your husband in a room full of windows. The brazen act left her sated as she collapsed into bed later that night with Mike.

"Have you heard from the groundskeeper?" Mike asked, half asleep.

"Who?"

"I guess this place comes with a groundskeeper. His salary and retirement were written into the will. He was supposed to meet us here today."

"No, I haven't gotten any calls. I'll see what I can find out tomorrow."

"You might stop down at his place. It's the little cottage on the other end of the lake. If you want me to go with you, we can go when I get back."

"All right," Callie said with a yawn. "I'm sure he probably just got the dates mixed up. I wanted to explore a little with Lizzy anyway; it will be a nice adventure."

"Well, you girls have fun. I wish I could join you, but I'm excited to meet with this banker tomorrow. He sounded excited about our meeting on his voicemail."

"Probably just another fan of the lore," Callie muttered, her eyes heavy.

Mike rolled over and kissed his wife before snuggling her into his arms. The pair dozed off into an exhausted sleep. Despite her body pleading for rest, Callie's mind refused to be at ease. She tossed and turned as dreams plagued her. A pounding had started to creep in, low at first, almost enough to be ignored. Yet the deeper she tried to move into REM, the more persistent the pounding became. Finally, after battling the protests of her subconscious, Callie stirred awake, determined to find the cause of the incessant pounding so sleep could claim her again.

The instant she was awake, fear gripped her heart as she frantically shoved Mike. He grumbled but came to as Callie screamed out his name, leaping to her feet. Sensing the urgency in her voice, Mike startled awake. Suddenly he understood what had gripped his wife with fear. Next to them, Lizzy was screaming in terror, a deafening pounding gripping the manor. He chased after his wife, fumbling with lights as they moved through the foreign house to the main staircase.

Callie's heart pounded, the fear in her daughter's screams piercing through every bone in her body. It was agony. Mike burst through her bedroom door, the lights flickering to life as they searched. She was nowhere in sight. Jerking open the closet doors, they looked at each other in terror as it dawned on them the yelling was now coming from somewhere else on the main floor. Racing through the house, the harrowing screams of their only child taunted them closer, Callie stumbling and busting open her toe as they ended up in the kitchen.

"Where is she, Mike?" Callie asked frantically.

She could feel the vibration now from the pounding. Wherever Lizzy was, she was trying frantically to escape. She screamed for her daughter, narrowing in on the girl's voice and the relief she felt when Lizzy responded.

31

"Here!" Mike screamed.

Callie followed his voice, finding a small hidden door outside the hall leading to the kitchen. There was no knob, only a small hole just large enough to fit an adult's finger inside. Mike was already tugging at it frantically as Lizzy sobbed and pleaded with him from the other side to hurry. He couldn't get a grip; something seemed to be wedged on the other side, keeping it from swinging open as one would assume it would.

"Quick! Get my toolbox and find the phillips head. I'm taking off the hinges," he yelled.

Callie raced to the front entrance, where she'd seen his box earlier in the day. Grabbing the tool, she darted back to her husband, assuring her daughter that they'd have her out soon. She had moved away from screaming to a helpless whimper Callie couldn't decipher, though the petrified sound of it had the potential to haunt her dreams. She prepared herself for the worst as Mike finally freed the door from its rusted hinges. Using the screwdriver, he pried at the door, yet still, her heart pounded in fear.

"Somethings wrong," Mike hissed. "The damn thing won't budge! It has to be locked from the other side."

She shook her head, refusing to accept what she could see with her own eyes. Shoving Mike to the side, Callie promised her daughter everything was fine. Her heart felt like it was in a press as she whispered to Lizzy, tugging and praying for the three-foot square of antique wood to give way. Behind them, footsteps moved, sending a chill down Callie's spine as she spun and saw nothing there.

6

---

deafening silence filled the manor as Lizzy stopped whimpering on the other side. Somehow it was worse than the sounds of despair. Callie talked to her daughter, pleaded with her to say something, but she struggled to even hear the faint sound of the girl breathing on the other side.

"Mike, Mike, you have to do something," she begged. "You have to get her out."

"Get back," he growled, taking several steps away from the door.

"Lizzy, get away from the door," Callie screamed.

Callie crawled backward, too worried for her daughter to risk standing and being just a few more feet away from her. Mike lunged for the door. His foot collided with a deafening sound, yet the oak wouldn't move for him. In a last desperate attempt, Callie tugged at the door one last time, pleading out loud for her daughter's safe return. The door lurched and gave way, sending Callie backward against the other side of the hallway. She held the small door in her hands for several seconds, too stunned to move until Lizzy emerged from the small space.

Her tear-streaked face snapped Callie from her shock as she scrambled forward, scooping her daughter into her arms and immediately taking her into the kitchen. She set the girl down on the island, looking her over for any wounds. When she found none, she let out a sigh of relief before the flood of emotions took over again. Her fear turned to worry and, finally, desperation to know what had been going through the little girl's mind.

"What were you doing in there, sweetheart?" Callie asked. "You had me and your father worried sick! What if we couldn't get you out? The fire department is twenty minutes away. We were so scared."

Callie pulled Lizzy into her arms again, afraid to let the child go even for a second. Her small arms wrapped around her mother, her body still trembling from the frightening experience. Suddenly, a wave of remorse coursed over Callie. Lizzy must have been terrified, just like she had been. Berating her with questions would only scare her more. She whispered softly to her daughter as she held her, promising her that everything would be okay.

Mike appeared in the hallway, motioning for Callie. She nodded and pulled away from Lizzy.

"Do you want some hot cocoa, honey?"

Lizzy nodded.

"Okay, why don't you go watch some cartoons, and I'll make us all three a cup."

"Okay, Mommy," Lizzy whimpered. "I'm sorry I went in there."

"It's okay, honey. We were just worried about you. Can you promise not to go in there again? Why don't you stay in your room from now on after we tuck you in?"

"I will, Mommy, I promise."

"Good, go watch some cartoons," Callie said as she lifted Lizzy off the countertop.

She poured a few cups of milk into a pot and set it on the stove on low. It was a frequent nighttime ritual of theirs, though it normally happened much earlier in the evening. With that done, Callie slipped into the hallway to find Mike kneeling outside the small space. There were a handful of items on the ground in front of him. The sight of the space's contents made Callie's stomach roll in a way she wasn't prepared for. He looked up when he saw Callie approach, handing her a ragged stuffed rabbit. It was covered in dust with one ear torn at the seams.

Callie could date it back at least seventy years from the faded paint on the animal's eyes. Her mother had been a collector of sorts for oddities such as the brown animal. Her eyes moved over the rest of the contents. A bouncy ball, paper airplane, and pirate's sword all pointed toward the items belonging to Mike's grandfather's foster son, Marcus. Why he'd had a stuffed animal so old, though, was still puzzling. Knowing that the items belonged to the now-deceased child sent a chill through Callie's spine.

"What the hell was she doing in there?" Mike asked.

Callie sighed, shaking her head as she slumped down against the wall. "I have no idea. She was so scared; I didn't want to press her. Jesus, how many other little places like that are we going to find here?"

"I have no idea, but I'm going to start looking tomorrow. The way sound carries in the house makes it damn near impossible to pinpoint where it's coming from."

"Or maybe the house just didn't want us to find her," Callie whispered.

Mike groaned. "Jesus, please don't start with that crap again. The house is fine. We just need to get familiar with it. I'll pick up the supplies tomorrow to board this off."

"No," Callie said quickly, shocking herself. "Now that we know it's here, I don't see any reason she can't play there. You'd have to find a way to keep it from locking on the inside again. What a terrible design."

"That's the thing, look at this," Mike said as he motioned for Callie to look at the space. "There's no lock on the inside. I think the wood just got jammed, but I don't know about keeping it accessible."

"Well, you already took the door off. What if we just kept it like it is? She can use it as a cubby, and we don't need to worry about her getting stuck again."

"Perfect," Mike said. "This is why I love you; you always think outside the box."

"Come have some cocoa with us," Callie offered.

"What do you want to do with this stuff?"

She frowned. "Just put it in the kitchen on top of the fridge for now. I'll box it up for the attic tomorrow with whatever else we find."

She rose to her feet, pulling Mike up with her. After a quick peck on the lips, he joined Lizzy on the couch as Callie worked on the drinks. The television was low enough that she could hear the duo talking about the cartoons they were watching. After a few minutes of silence, Mike asked Lizzy how she managed to find the space. Callie held her breath, not daring to make a noise as she listened for her daughter's reply.

"My friend showed me," Lizzy replied.

"Oh? Your friend?" Mike pressed. "Have we met this friend before?"

She giggled. "Of course not, Daddy. You know that you and Mom can't see my special friends."

Callie let out the breath she'd been holding. Another imaginary friend. They came and went regularly. It made sense. It had been a few days since the last one, Marybeth, had left. Last year, when they'd first started showing up, Callie had asked the hospital's resident psychologist about them. He'd assured her that it was perfectly normal, especially for a child who wasn't in daycare full time. Sometimes, they made bonds with other kids their own age who weren't there. "Nothing to worry about," he'd told her.

"A new friend, huh? A boy, too; that's new," Mike offered.

"He's different," Lizzy said casually. "He's not like my other friends."

"He's not? How is he different? Is it because he's a boy?"

She shrugged. "I don't know, Daddy. I don't know anything about boys. They have cooties, you know."

Mike chuckled. "I know they do. Well, if you figure out how he's different, you let me know. So, he showed you the crawlspace, huh? I suppose he talked you into getting out of bed to find it, too?"

"He said he knows all sorts of places in the house. He lived here, too, you know."

"Wow, sounds like your imagination is really going wild with this one."

"They aren't pretend, Dad. Don't you know anything?"

"Sorry," Mike muttered, properly chagrined. "I think maybe the next time you and your new friend want to do something, you should ask Mom or me first, okay?"

"Okay, Daddy, I will, I promise. I was just excited to see everything."

"We've got lots of time to explore," he promised her.

Callie came round with three mugs on a tray. Lizzy jumped forward, grateful for the drink as she lay back and sipped it. Mike took his in one hand, wrapping the other around Callie's shoulder as she sat next to him. Their first night at the manor wasn't turning out as he'd planned. Things were going to take some time to adjust to. Hopefully, after they went back to bed, they'd be able to get to sleep. With Lizzy's promise not to leave her room again, they finished their drinks and headed back upstairs to tuck her in.

Mike knew Callie was hesitant to leave Lizzy alone again, but he managed to get her back to the bedroom after a few protests. Lizzy hadn't even made it through her cocoa before passing out in his arms. There was no way she'd be awake again before the morning. Finally, Callie relented and followed him back to their bedroom, where she collapsed into bed. He couldn't bring himself to sleep, not yet. For several minutes, he watched his wife toss and turn before he finally succumbed to a restless night of strange dreams.

7

"*D*id you get any sleep last night?" Mike asked.

Callie shook her head. "A little bit, I just had weird dreams. Nothing I want to talk about. It just threw me for a loop."

"Well, it looks like Lizzy is catching up on some sleep after that fiasco."

"Did you—"

"I checked on her five minutes ago before I came downstairs. She's in bed, breathing, and even snoring a little bit. Her door's cracked open so you can hear her, too. Do you want me to pick up a baby monitor while I'm in town?"

"No," Callie mumbled. "I won't say the idea didn't cross my mind, but she'd hate that. I'll keep a lookout for any more crawl spaces while I'm unpacking today. It's going to take a week just to get the first layer of dust off everything here."

"Well, make an inventory of any damages you see

while you're at it. I have a feeling this place is going to have all sorts of little tricks up its sleeve."

"Careful, you're starting to sound like me."

"Just don't go giving this house more credit than it deserves. It's going to keep us busy, though."

"I can handle busy, just no more late-night scares like that."

"Agreed, will you give Lizzy a kiss for me? My meeting is at ten. I want to walk around a little in town and get my bearings before I see the bank manager."

"Of course," Callie said, giving Mike a kiss.

She watched him disappear out the front door. Before long, a cloud of dust was all she could see along the driveway. Turning her attention back to the plethora of boxes piling into the kitchen from the front parlor, Callie started lifting and moving them to their designated rooms. After a few minutes, she came across the one containing Mike's laptop and writing supplies. It had gone untouched since their meeting with Benjamin's attorney weeks ago. Her heart lurched, wondering how long it would be before he started typing again. Tucked beneath it were the rejection letters. It was a morbid that writers saved such things.

Making her way up the steps, she paused at the top to listen for Lizzy's snoring just a few doors down. When the familiar sound filled her ears, she continued down the hall in the opposite direction. The study door creaked with foreboding as she pushed it open. It hadn't been cleaned as carefully as Lizzy's room. She could still pick up the faint traces of industrial cleanser. Likewise, the wear pattern on the floor showed polished wood where a rug once sat beneath the heavy poplar desk. Callie had seen enough in her line of work to know the blood would never come out of the fabric; the groundskeeper had burned it, no doubt.

It felt wrong to be in the space. It was dark and uninviting. Callie wasn't surprised her husband loved it. The history of the room alone was enough to make a writer drool. Setting the box onto the desk, a cloud of dust wafted into the air. It caught the light as she pulled back the aged curtains, a strong beam knocking away the lingering depression that filled the room. With the sunlight now reflecting through the glass, the space was truly remarkable. One entire wall was a bookshelf that recessed back into the wall. She ran her fingers along the books, making note of several titles she hadn't see outside of museums before.

Everything about the house had mystery. She sat back in the antique chair and pulled open the top set of drawers, revealing a thick stack of leather-bound journals. They must have cost the old man a fortune. Before she could open the first one, she felt someone watching her. Looking up, Callie jumped when she saw a figure standing at the door—Lizzy. Letting out a sigh of relief, she jumped to her feet and circled back around the desk to scoop her daughter into her arms.

"I didn't hear you wake up, honey. How did you sleep?"

"Okay," Lizzy muttered. She'd never been much of a morning person. "What are you doing in here? You aren't supposed to be in Mr. Grant's study."

"Oh yeah?" Callie asked. "Never mind all that, are you hungry. Do you want some breakfast?"

Lizzy nodded as Callie set her down, closing the study door behind them as they started for the kitchen. A few minutes later, Lizzy was settled at the island, coloring as she ate cereal. Callie listened to her talking with her new imaginary friend as she unpacked more boxes in the kitchen. An hour passed without a word from Mike, making her nervous despite knowing it could take several hours to get through all the paperwork. She tried to distract herself with the boxes while Lizzy moved on to watch cartoons. It was a beautiful day outside. She'd promised her they would explore right after lunch, leaving Callie just a few hours to get work done.

With the kitchen ready to go, she moved on to the master bedroom. They'd been sure to do all their laundry before leaving. The plumbing in the house was questionable, and they needed to buy a washer and dryer anyway. While Callie worked at hanging clothes, her mind trailed back to the journals she'd found earlier. She'd known Benjamin had an affection for writing, but from what she'd seen, it was almost an obsession, much like Mike. There'd been at least ten in the drawer. Callie would bet her left hand that they were only the start of his stories.

Desperate to get back into the office and learn more about the former owner of the manor, she quickly finished the last two boxes in the bedroom and popped into the kitchen. Lizzy remained content with cartoons, coloring, and her strange new imaginary friend. Slipping past the little girl unnoticed, she crossed back to the stair-

43

case and into the study, leaving the door cracked so she could hear Lizzy long before she made it to the door again. Just as she'd suspected, two more drawers were full of journals. Looking at the spines, she found the very first journal dated over three decades prior.

It was nothing interesting, despite its age and flawless penmanship. He'd made note of the assets he had, various pieces of art he'd come to collect, and a little about his wife's cooking. Closing it again, Callie slid it back into its spot and moved to another drawer, the dates for it starting ten years before. She was captivated for a split second before hearing Lizzy giggle downstairs. Her phone vibrated on the desk, making her jump. Mike had texted, the meeting was getting underway. Her heart raced, listening to Lizzy talking to herself downstairs. Their entire future rode on what the bank manager said to Mike.

This whole town is breathing down my neck now with her gone. I don't know why I'd want to stay. Hell, I don't know why I'd sell them anything after the way they treated us. I might just give it all to some hippies; see how those damned fools like the land then....

Callie chucked at Benjamin's writing. It was obvious there had been interest in the property. She could only assume he was referring to his wife as the woman who was gone. The more she read, the more she found herself wrapped up in the history of it all. Her innate sense of curiosity had always come at a cost. Mike didn't want anything to do with the Grant legacy, yet Callie could see the good in knowing the people whose lives they were taking over by staying at the manor.

Then next time one of them sets foot on the property, I've got half a mind to send them right to their maker. I'll let God sort them out and claim self-defense. This country isn't worth a darn anymore anyway. It's a wonder they haven't sold their souls yet to get their grubby paws on my lake.

As much as she wanted to linger in the office and read, she didn't like being so far from Lizzy after the night's events. Grabbing the journal, she tucked it under her arm and slipped out of the office, closing the door behind her. She paused at the top of the steps, listening to Lizzy tell her imaginary friend all about how much fun the move had been and how she missed her friends but she was excited to make new ones. Callie had one foot on the steps when she heard Lizzy ask if the newest imaginary character would be her friend.

"You bet," a man replied.

The journal tumbled from Callie's hands onto the stairs, her heart pounding as the hair on the back of her neck stood on end.

8

*S*he skidded to a stop at the sight of the man standing dangerously close to her daughter. Thankfully, the child was blissfully unaware of the risk as she chatted with him about what she was drawing. She didn't hear her mother arrive, but the man did. He glanced up, towering over her 5'4" frame by at least ten inches. He looked about her age, though the years had obviously taken their toll on him. Her hands were shaking as her mind raced, trying to find any way that she could get to her endangered daughter before the man had a chance to react.

"Lizzy, get over here, right now," Callie whispered.

Lizzy froze, her eyes landing on her mother. The tone in her voice demanded immediate action. Thankfully, the little girl listened for a change and darted to her side, unscathed. Callie wrapped one arm protectively around her daughter and glared at the man. He stepped forward, extending a hand though she shrank away from him.

Sensing her fear, he froze and lifted up his hands in a show of surrender. It did little to ease Callie's mind. They were just a few feet from the door now. If they made a run for it, perhaps they'd escape his clutches.

"Hey, there, sorry for just coming in like that. I didn't think anyone was here."

"Who are you?"

"Name's Frank. I was old Ben's caretaker. Listen, I'm real sorry. The front door was open, and I heard her in here talking to someone. I guess I should have put two and two together."

"We were expecting you yesterday," Callie said, still not at ease.

"Yeah, I don't know what happened there. I must have got my dates mixed up. I was up visiting my daughter. She just had her first baby."

Callie pursed her lips. She knew the door was closed when she went upstairs. You didn't live in New York City without making sure your home was secure. It was impossible to miss the distinct sound of it being locked, the ancient mechanisms bumping and grinding when the key was turned. The noise had scared her at first, but she knew Mike had locked the door when he had left. Hopefully, he would be back soon. The man standing in front of her still made her stomach churn. It wasn't that she didn't believe his story; there just seemed to be something off about him.

He reached into his pocket, making her take another step backward. Frank pulled a phone out of his pocket, scrolling through a set of pictures of a newborn. It was easy to see he'd been telling the truth about visiting his daughter. Perhaps he wasn't her age and managed to take amazing care of himself. After a few more tense moments, Callie let go of Lizzy, and she darted back to her coloring book. At least now, Frank was closer to Callie than he was Lizzy. She glared at him, unsure of what her next move should be. She'd never had a groundskeeper before.

"Listen, I really didn't mean to startle you. I figured you'd be right in the door, what with it open and all that. The doorbell hasn't worked in months. I always mean to get it fixed, but Ben was funny about things like that toward the end there."

Callie's eyes darted to Lizzy. "You knew him?"

"Course I did. I worked for Ben for my entire life. My family and his go way back. Hell, he employed my father, too. I owe him everything. I sure was shocked to find out he left me in the will, though."

"He left you enough to take an early retirement on, didn't he?"

"Sure did, but I couldn't do that to this place. Maybe once we get you all set up, I'll think about it."

"That's a pretty generous move for people you don't know."

"Of course, I know you all. You're family, just like Ben was. Naw, I'd feel plum awful if I left you three to fend for yourself."

"Well then, I guess we can start by going over the house. Is there anything we should know about it? Bad foundation, broken windows, that sort of thing?"

Frank shrugged and looked around the house. For the

first time, Callie saw a brief flicker of something else behind his eyes, but it was gone as quickly as it appeared. The moment was so brief, she couldn't decipher if it was fear or anger, possibly a little of both. Yet, he'd brought up a valid point. There was a ton of things they didn't know about the property. With Mike's dream of turning it into a bed and breakfast, Frank's knowledge could be useful.

"It's just another old house, I reckon. I come from a superstitious lot, can't put much stake in what I say if you believe the townsfolk."

Callie's attention perked up. "What sort of superstitions?"

"Well now, I don't think you should concern yourself with old tales like that. Why don't we just settle on the porch, and I can let you know what I know about the house?"

"Sure," she muttered, a little deflated.

They walked outside, sitting back in the aged wicker for several minutes of awkward silence. The questions were racing through her mind. They all seemed to sound crazy, though. It wouldn't do her any good to scare off the one man who knew Benjamin. She strummed her fingers impatiently as he told her about the house's wiring and what needed to be done. For the most part, it was all information they already knew. The inspector had done a thorough, if not depressing, job of filling them in. At one point, she was sure the man would tell them it was better off up in flames.

"It sounds like you and Benjamin were close," Callie pressed. "I'm sorry for your loss."

"I made my peace with his death long before he was in the ground," Frank muttered.

"So it's true that he wasn't all there in the head?"

"He had a hard lot in life. I don't think he ever expected to go out like that."

"But he killed himself; you can't really blame that on anyone else."

"Didn't say I was. I know what people say he did. Hell, I was the one who found him, and…well, I found all three of them. A man like Benjamin, though, he could have been losing his mind and never would have gotten help."

Silence filled the humid air once again. Callie could see how distraught the line of questioning had made Frank. Guilt washed over her. Perhaps the nuns in school had been right and she didn't know when to let things go. What would they say about the strange noises and eerie nature of the manor, though? Her gut wanted to press on for answers, but the softness of her heart won the battle in the end.

"I'm sorry, I'm way out of line. You know my husband should be home soon if you want to talk to him. He knows so much more about the property already than I do."

"He's Benjamin's grandson, right? At least that's the rumor going around town. I didn't get to sit in on the reading of the will, what with being out of town and all."

"Right," Callie muttered. "You didn't miss much. My husband is hoping to turn this place into a bed and breakfast. I'm sure he's going to want to keep you on as long as you'd like to stay."

"Ben's grandson?" Frank repeated.

"Yes. Although I should warn you, the two weren't close. If you are looking for any sort of bond between the men, they didn't even know each other."

"I know that. Hell, I didn't know about your husband until after Ben was already passed. He kept that little nugget to himself."

"I really don't know why we're here," Callie admitted. "I never in a million years thought we would end up here. Even as we were pulling up yesterday, it didn't feel real."

"Well, you're here. Guess it doesn't really matter what you planned before that; the manor has you now."

Callie didn't like the ominous tone in his voice, but she didn't say anything. He'd made it abundantly clear that his opinions on the property weren't going to be shared with her easily. Callie was going to need to befriend Frank to unravel the mysteries of Grant Manor. Thankfully, without a job and with most of the unpacking already done, she had nothing but time on her hands as they listened to Lizzy talking away inside to her imaginary friend.

The wind moved through the trees. Despite the warm temperatures, Callie felt a chill before glancing at Lizzy through the massive bay windows. For a split second, she swore she saw a small figure sitting next to her daughter. The wind shifted, and she blinked, the figure gone once again, just a figment of her imagination.

9

"*I* suppose I should get unpacked and let you folks get settled in," Frank said. "Just let me know if you need help with anything. I'll be doing the lawn this week, but I'm handy around the house as well."

"Thank you, I get the feeling we'll need all hands on deck for this place. It certainly has its own vibes."

"That's one way of putting it," he muttered.

Callie pursed her lips. Instinct told her the man had stronger opinions about the estate than he was letting on. She didn't want to push him, but at the same time, her family had left everything behind to try to run the property. If something was going on with Frank, she needed to know. Her stomach lurched. Why couldn't he just take the retirement Benjamin had left for him? Instead, he was welcome to stay on with the property as long as he liked, making him more of a burden than a blessing.

"You don't seem to be very fond of Grant Manor. If

you don't mind my asking, why are you staying on?" Callie asked.

Frank looked out over the property and smiled. "Because this place is my home. She might be evil, but she's all I've got left with Benjamin and the kids gone."

Callie's heart lurched. She'd taken his evasive nature all wrong. For the first time, she saw the wounded man who had lost his family. His words played on a loop in her mind.

"You think the house is evil?" Callie whispered.

"I probably shouldn't have said that, but I like you well enough. This place, I reckon that's what killed old Ben. It drove him mad. It does that to people."

She swallowed. "You were the one who found them, weren't you?"

He nodded, his gaze never leaving the tree line. "Yes, ma'am. I was the one who buried them, too, out at the old family plot. Bastards at the morgue wouldn't let me make the boxes myself, something about the damned environment."

"My God, that must have been awful for you. I'm so sorry."

"Don't be," he grumbled, his tone dropping. "Doesn't do anyone any good. You can't change the past...but you can change the future."

"Well, that's why we're here," Callie said, ignoring the ominous tone in Frank's voice. "We want to make this place something wonderful."

"I wish you all the best of luck then. You're going to need it."

"Actually, all we need is a positive attitude right now. I hope you'll think about that when you're working around here. Lizzy is young and influential. I don't want her knowing about what happened at the manor," Callie hissed.

Frank's eyes snapped to her. "I won't tell her a thing, but you better watch her."

"Are you threatening—"

"Of course not!" he snapped. "This house has a way of—"

"Yes, I heard you the first time. If my only worry is your superstitions, then I don't think I'm too concerned. If you'll excuse me, I need to get back to work."

"Of course, if you need me, I'm just a phone call away."

"I'm sure my husband will want to talk to you when he gets home. This is his project; he'll have more details for you."

"I look forward to meeting him," Frank said.

Callie watched him hobble down the steps. She didn't wait long before heading inside and closing the door firmly behind her. After feeling the wind on the porch, though, she was almost able to convince herself it was strong enough to blow open the heavy door. Frank's words still lingered in her ears despite trying to distract herself by unpacking more boxes. The house felt too small, isolated from the rest of the world. It was near suffocating for her.

"Hey! Let's go explore," she said to Lizzy, plastering a smile on her face.

Lizzy jumped up immediately, running to the steps

and tugging on her shoes before darting out onto the porch. It was easy to forget about her encounter with Frank once they were in the woods. Lizzy's excitement was a cure for anyone's anxiety. She didn't let anything hold her back. It was hard to imagine Callie was looking at the same girl who had been terrified the night before. All the evening's event seemed to be forgotten by Lizzy, thank God.

It wasn't long before the pair came to a clearing, and Callie's unease returned. The pristine landscaping felt out of place in the thick of the brush and towering maple trees. Yet, it was obvious someone took exceptional care of the space. Callie watched Lizzy run enthusiastically up to a tall stone wall. It towered over Callie by at least two feet. A heavy wrought iron gate skewed the walls contents. Lizzy grabbed the handle just as Callie reached her, quickly keeping the door closed.

"Mommy, I want to see what's in there."

"I know, but we don't just go barging into places without an adult. Do you understand me? That's what got you into trouble last night as well," Callie reminded her.

Lizzy blushed. "I'm sorry, Mommy. I just got excited. Do you think we can look inside?"

"Well," Callie frowned, "it's on our property, so I don't see why not. You have to listen to me once we are inside, though, okay?"

"Okay!" Lizzy agreed excitedly.

Callie tugged open the door, her heart sinking as she caught a glimpse of the border's contents through the narrow slits in the black iron. It was too late to stop, though; Lizzy had already gasped. She knew they were walking into a small cemetery. There were fifteen headstones, with the first two rows consisting of six each, yet the third had only three. That trio stuck out against the rest of the scenery. The newly sprung grass lacked the aged lushness that covered the rest of the mounds. Stone benches sat on either side of the entrance while carefully manicured flowerbeds lined the walls. Had it not been for the new graves, Callie would have relished the cemetery's serenity.

Lizzy was content looking around as Callie went from one headstone to the next. Every last name was the same, Grant. Even those daughters who had gone on to get married were buried with their maiden name. Though it was evident that their husbands didn't make it into the family plot. Sons were different. Their spouses and children lay next to them beneath Callie's feet. She couldn't help but notice there were only three more plots left before the cemetery was out of space. At the end of the second row, she paused, unsure if she wanted to continue to the final three markers. She couldn't be sure what had happened to the others who had met their demise. Knowing that a Grant had killed his wards was different.

Morbid curiosity pushed her forward. She read Benjamin's first. Considering how things had ended, it was highly anti-climactic. Obviously, he'd instructed them before his death on what to put. The children were different, though. No one could imagine planning something like that. Her eyes shot to Lizzy, now cheerfully talking to her imaginary friend as they sat on one of the benches near the entrance. Vera had been the older twin. Below her birthday and death date was a single sentence.

She loved to sing, and now her song will never end.

Callie quickly moved to the final headstone as she tried to decipher Vera's.

A trickster to the end. Hide and seek world champion.

"Mommy! Can we go now? He doesn't like it here," Lizzy yelled.

Callie jumped at the sound of her daughter's voice. She'd almost forgotten the girl was there. Quickly turning away from the headstones, she made her way back to Lizzy. Carefully closing the gate behind her, Callie took Lizzy's hand as they wandered back down the path. Her daughter walked silently next to her. For a child who rarely stopped talking, it was strange behavior.

"Honey, are you okay? Did the cemetery scare you?" Callie asked.

Lizzy shook her head. "No, not me. My friend."

"Ah, well, that's okay, honey, even if it was you who was scared. Sometimes, places like that can seem frightening."

"He wasn't scared, Mommy. He's been there before. That's how I knew where to go, silly."

Callie's stomach lurched. "Oh, he has?"

"Yes, Mommy, that's where he lives. He wanted us to come and see, but he doesn't like it there."

"That doesn't sound like a very nice place for a little boy to live."

"He used to live in the house…but not anymore, " Lizzy muttered.

MARIE WILKENS

"Lizzy," Callie started, her voice barely a whisper, "what's your friend's name?"

Lizzy rolled her eyes. "You already know that, Mommy. You just saw it! I'm only six and I can read, you know."

"Lizzy, what's his name?" Callie asked again.

"Marcus, Mommy…"

Lizzy continued to talk about her imaginary friend, but Callie wasn't listening. The color had drained from her cheeks. Each step felt like she was walking in a dream. The fear that had been suffocating her the night before returned. Was her daughter's friend imaginary at all?

"*B*oy, I must say, it's a downright pleasure to meet you, young man," the banker said.

Mike grinned, slightly shocked by the warm greeting and firm handshake alike. It was refreshing to finally meet someone who seemed pleased he was there. Just moments before at the hardware store, an older woman had nearly fainted when she learned who his father was. The entire community seemed to enjoy living in another era, one wrought with bigotry and prejudice. He'd never been more proud of both his fathers in his life. Unfortunately, it had put him in a bad temper right before the big meeting. As they sat down in the man's office, Mike eased some.

"Look at me," the banker grinned. "So tickled that I didn't even introduce myself. I'm Collin Albright, manager here at Third National Bank."

"Michael Grant," he replied. "It's a pleasure to meet

you. I have to say, I was a little surprised you wanted to handle this personally."

"I have to admit, I've had an interest in the Grant estate my entire life. You don't grow up in this town and not know about it."

"Well, it's definitely something I think the public should get more of. That's why I'm here today. I'd like to apply for a loan to fix the place up and turn it into a bed and breakfast."

"Wow! That's fantastic! Now I did look over your application. You've got everything we need, and with your wife's credit, a loan is no problem. I have to ask, though, you two don't seem like the small-town type."

Mike burst into laughter. "We aren't, not by any stretch of the imagination. We both loved New York, but the cost of living there is insane. This is a free house and a fresh start. So you think we'll be approved?"

"Without question," Collin said. "Why don't you just sell the place instead? I'd be happy to take it off your hands at one hell of a fair price."

Mike chuckled again. "Trust me, if it were that easy, we wouldn't be down here. Apparently, my grandfather had it written into the will that it can't be sold. I never knew the guy, but I don't think we would have gotten along very well."

"Benjamin Grant was a stubborn man, that's for sure," Collin said.

"That seems to be what everyone thinks, but again, I didn't know him at all and definitely not well enough to pass judgment. I'm sure if there had been any other living relative, the property would have gone to them. My father and Benjamin weren't exactly close."

"It's a wonder. Everyone thought that boy was dead. Your showing up here sure has people's tongues wagging."

"Yeah, I got that feeling. I don't know why people hate me so much for wanting to make a go of the property. You'd think it would mean more money for the town. Isn't that a good thing?"

"Don't worry, son, they'll come around. I think people were hoping the property would go to the county after your grandfather's passing. You being here, hell, you existing at all, sure threw this town for a loop."

"Well, I'm sorry everyone's so disappointed it won't be going to the city. I guess there isn't much I can do about it except show them we're going to be a good asset to the community."

Collin smiled, though Mike felt a bit like he was being placated. It drove him nuts to know everyone disliked them. All he wanted was what was best for his small family. In the few hours he'd been in town, Mike was starting to wonder if moving to Grant Manor was a mistake. He sat in awkward silence as Collin started shuffling through the paperwork on his desk. When he turned it around and handed Mike a pen, Mike was shocked.

"This is three times what we asked for," he stammered.

Collin shrugged. "Your wife has exceptional credit. Now when I tried to run it with both your names, you didn't come close to that number."

Mike blushed. "Yeah, I haven't always been great with money."

"It doesn't matter now. The house's assets, assuming they are still there, would cover this amount ten times over. I'd hate to see you get rid of pieces, though. They have such a history! If this money helps hang onto them, I'm happy to stick my neck out."

"I think I'll have to talk to my wife first. We agreed on the loan, but not that much. I don't think we could ever use—"

"Nonsense. Running the forms again will just lower her score more. Just use what you need and save the rest for a rainy day. You have her power of attorney, correct?"

"Yeah, but—"

"Then I don't see any reason you shouldn't be walking out of here with almost half a million dollars in your pocket. Do you?"

Mike frowned. It was a ridiculous sum. Even with the two small items they'd sold off, the house's assets could cover the loan many times, just like the bank manager had stated. Still, it wasn't the amount he and Callie had agreed on. He looked down at his phone, contemplating if he should call her. Getting her to agree to the loan had taken days, a change like this and they might miss their shot altogether. Taking a deep breath, Mike grabbed the pen and quickly scribbled his signature on every page Collin had marked. A few minutes later, he was leaving the bank with more money in their newly opened joint account than he could ever dream of.

Still, he took his time on the drive home, trying to come up with the best approach to tell Callie about the extra padding in the loan. It wouldn't be enough to use Collin's argument. Mike knew he should have called her, but he had made a decision. Callie always told him he needed to go for what he wanted; now was as good a time as any to start listening to her. Still, he stopped at the end of the driveway. He'd noticed the gates that afternoon and promised himself he'd rip down the snaking vines on his way back.

He didn't see the shadow on the other side as he climbed out. Donning his new work gloves, he started to tug at the hearty brown veins. One by one, they came tumbling down, Mike dodging out of the way at every turn but still not fast enough to miss a few of the long tendrils. Suddenly, he felt hands behind him, pulling at the flora as well. A man gave a disgruntled curse as Mike was freed at last from the vines.

"Jesus!" Mike exclaimed, stumbling back. "Those things could kill a man! Thanks for that, pal."

"Any time. The name's Frank. Judging by the color of your hair, I'd guess your Benjamin's boy?"

Mike nodded. "You're the groundskeeper, I take it?"

Frank nodded. "Sure am. I already met the missus and little one. Noticed the overgrowth when I got in this morning."

"Well, I'd like to get this place as pretty as it was back in its heyday. If we can turn a profit, I know everything will be okay."

"That's a tall order," Frank grumbled. "I suppose it can be done, though. It'll take a well of money and about as much manpower as the two of us can handle, assuming you're not afraid of a little elbow grease. The missus mentioned you're from New York?"

Mike laughed. "Don't judge me just yet, friend. I spent the summers working on my grandparents' farm in upstate. I've known my fair share of labor. Now, I can't say I know much beyond the grunt work, but if you point me at a task and tell me what needs to be done, I'll do my best."

"That's all you can ask for in a boss," Frank said with a grin. "Honestly, I think I might have frightened your old lady a touch. That house has a mind of its own. She sure seemed a little shaken."

Mike sighed. "Don't worry too much about her. She's got a habit of letting her imagination run wild when it comes to ghost stories. I'm sure she's already making up a whole plot for the tale in her mind. She'll come around eventually."

"What do you say we get this brush down, then I can show you the machine shop and tractors. Might be able to get it all cleared out and have a fire later on."

Mike grinned. "Sounds perfect. Lizzy would love that. Plus, Callie can't get mad if I'm working on the manor."

"Oh yeah? You in deep water already? You two seem too young to have too much on your shoulders."

"I take it you've never been married before?" Mike asked.

Frank shook his head. "Can't say I've ever had the pleasure."

"Just remember to always carry a dozen roses and a box of chocolates with you. Otherwise, get used to sleeping on the sofa!"

11

"*I* can't believe you!" Callie hissed. "Did you even stop to think about how I would feel about all this?"

"Sweetheart, it's like Collin said, we don't have to spend it all. Whatever we use, we'll just put toward the payments. It's just a safety net."

"The safety net was supposed to be the assets. Now, if you blow through that money, we lose everything and my credit is shot to boot!"

Color jumped to Mike's cheeks. Instantly, Callie regretted the way she had worded things, but her anger continued to seep through. Of course, he hadn't thought it through. Mike was so easy to talk into things. She blamed herself for not going with him. Still, never in a million years would she have guessed the bank would offer them so much. After all, they were just a young couple with almost no collateral. Well, except for the manor that was now at stake. Her stomach rolled. They couldn't lose everything, not after all they'd given up to get there.

"Mike—"

"No, I get it. I fuck up everything. I guess that's just what I do. I wish I could tell you this time will be different, but it sounds like you've already decided for me that I'm going to screw it up."

"I didn't mean it like that," Callie muttered. "I'm sorry, Mike. It was just a shock, is all. That's a lot of money to have just sitting around, and from the sound of things, he was pretty excited to take that lien on the manor."

"It's on the assets, not the manor. I haven't spent any of it yet, you know. We can always go back tomorrow and undo it if you want."

She shook her head. "No. I trust you. Please, just be careful with our future, okay?"

"I will, I promise you. You've always supported me; I won't let you down," Mike assured her. "What do you think about skipping cooking tonight and ordering takeout? Collin said they get delivery out here."

"Really?" Callie mused. "I guess that's a perk of a small town. You'd never get delivery five miles away in the city. I've just got two more boxes to move into the basement. Do you want to order? Dealers choice."

"Chinese it is. I'll get Lizzy into the tub afterward. You take care of whatever you need."

Callie kissed Mike's cheek and grabbed the first box. Had she asked, Mike would have brought the Christmas ornaments down to the basement for her. She was enjoying getting familiar with the house, though, and ultimately, it would be her pulling them back out to decorate in a few months. If she could ease some of the load on his shoulders, she'd do so willingly every time. The light leading down the rickety steps flickered to life after a couple firm tugs. She carefully dodged an exposed nail at the base of the steps and made a mental note to have Mike pull it tomorrow.

She had to set down the box to locate the single bulb that would give her lighting in the musty space. It, too, struggled to come to life. In every room of the house, she seemed to stumble upon more and more issues. It was impossible to know how old the wiring throughout really was. Some of it appeared so brittle, it could be crushed between a strong set of fingers. Behind her, in the dark corners the light couldn't reach, something scurried across the floor.

She picked up the box slowly, her eyes watching the corner where the noise had come from, but it didn't happen again. After a few seconds of heavy silence, she let out the breath she'd been holding and continued toward the shelving near the back wall of the basement. Her heart froze before her feet did when a new sound came from somewhere closer, sounding as though it was right behind her.

It was the telltale sound of a child's laughter. Her mind darted to Lizzy's friend, Marcus. Had it been a boy or a girl? Did it matter? She closed her eyes. It was in her head. It was just in her head. The house was old and had a personality of its own. Callie tried to move and set the box on the shelf, but her body was frozen in place. The battle between her mind and the fear crippling it was in full force, waging silently inside her.

The curse, the curse persisted still...

She gasped, the lyrical voice faint behind her as the box dropped from her grip. The glass inside shattered as it fell to the floor. Callie spun around. The scurry of rodents she could handle, but not a child's voice singing, especially given the circumstances. She swallowed, her throat dry as the light overhead threatened to blow. Each flicker seemed to bring the danger closer, unseen but malice in its origins all the same. Something was wrong with the house. Why didn't Mike believe her?

"Whose there?" Callie stammered, her voice low. "Is someone there?"

The women all gone, gone from the will...

A sob slipped past her lips, a mixture of pure fear and inexplicable dread that seemed to fill the very air she breathed. Her chest constricted despite no change in her movement. Closing her eyes, Callie tried desperately to convince her mind that it was just their imagination. Nothing was lurking in the darkness except a few stray mice and perhaps some spiders. Yet the dread wouldn't leave, nor would the sensation that she was being watched. It took all her self-control to crack open her eyes just a little, fully expecting to see a hideous monster of untold origins staring back at her.

There was nothing in front of her but the shattered remains of her ornaments, slipping out on the dusty floor, giving the illusion of water shimmering beneath her feet. The breath she'd been holding in fear finally eased. There was nothing in the basement but her and the shattered remains of their ancient holiday decorations. With a heavy sigh, she bent down and started picking up the bigger shards of glass. The rest would need a broom. Silently, she cursed herself for being so jumpy. It was amazing how much a strange location could distort your senses.

"Honey?" Mike called down. "Are you okay?"

"Yes," she yelled back. "I just spooked myself and dropped the damn ornaments."

"Do you need help cleaning up?" he asked, one foot already on the steps.

"No, I'm fine. I'm going to come up and deal with it tomorrow," she muttered.

"All right. Lizzy and I are going to go check on the ducks by the pond. You sure you are okay?"

"Yeah," she promised. "I'm right behind you."

"Okay," he said.

She listened to his footsteps falling farther away as she set off for the bottom of the steps again. The basement had given her enough of a bad vibe that she just wanted to get out of there. When she reached the stairs, she glanced back at the gently swaying bulb and groaned. Had it been their apartment complex's basement facility, she would have let it glowing. At least there, she could rest easy, knowing a faulty wire wouldn't burn the place down. At Grant Manor, though, it seemed like anything was possible. The light flickered, cementing her decision that it was better to be safe than sorry, despite the minor thrill she got at the idea of watching the house burn to the ground.

Callie closed the distance between her and the light quickly, not wanting to linger in the basement. As soon as she pulled the string, darkness encompassed her. The sole light at the top of the steps now seemed dim and far away as she started back for the steps once again. There was no denying the sensation of being watched from the shadows. It sent a shudder coursing through Callie's body. The light at the top of the staircase flickered, momentarily wrapping her in a complete blackout. The brief few seconds were all it took for her to see the flash of two figures lurking near the base of the steps. Small figures. She skidded to a stop and gasped, her heart racing so fast she thought she'd pass out.

When the light finally returned, there was nothing at the base of the steps but a gathering of dust. Callie was sure of what she had seen, though. The knots that had formed in her stomach had only ever appeared when something was terribly wrong. It was the same sensation she'd gotten while pregnant with Lizzy. At five months, she'd gone into preterm labor. The doctors had called her quick reaction time a stroke of luck thanks to her medical training. Yet Callie knew that none of her years of study could have prepared her for what a mother's instinct already knew—her child was in danger.

12
_____

*C*allie's mind dove into survival mode, her body flushing with adrenaline as her eyes darted around the space once more. The dim light now filled the space, though she could still feel the hairs on the nape of her neck standing on end. There was something down there with her. No hallucination nor active imagination could account for what she'd just seen. Likewise, she knew who the children were who seemed determined to drive Callie and her family from Grant Manor. Callie's stomach rolled as she swallowed, the dry air doing little to help ease her trepidations as her eyes darted to the top of the steps.

"Please come back, Mike, please," she whispered.

No sounds greeted her save for the old estate's struggling pipes as the washer started to fill in the laundry room above her. Callie didn't remember starting it, but the rushing water moved through the pipes with a deafening sound. The chunks of rust reminded her of a wind chime as they moved down the pipe. There was no time to yell for help, nor any reason. Mike was too far away from the house. Thankfully, Lizzy was with him. At least Callie knew her daughter wasn't upstairs, alone and frightened with the spirits who seemed to hate the entire clan.

The light flickered, shoving Callie's fear back to the surface. There was no chance in hell she was going to stay down there with the monsters. When the aged light gave one final wane, she darted for the base of the steps again, not stopping until she reached them. Cool air moved across her as she passed the spot where the spirits had been just a few minutes before. Just as she took the first step, something grabbed at the hem of her dress. The putrid smell of rotting flesh filled her nose. She struggled not to gag, but her instinct kicked in before she could stop herself. She turned to see what had grabbed her. Nothing.

"It's in your head, Callie," she reminded herself. "It's just in your head."

Her words seemed to goad the spirits as two small but distinguishable, invisible hands shoved her forward. Above her, the ominous sound of the water running had ground to a halt, now replaced with something new, something somehow even worse. A subtle step, followed by a delicate dragging. Callie caught herself just as the steps collided with her knees, the sound above her moving closer to the top of the stairs. Pulling one foot off the ground, she scrambled for the top, a surprising jolt of pain searing her calf as she did. Callie screamed out in agony but didn't stop.

Leave...leave now... a child's voice whispered.

Callie's heart was beating so hard, she could feel the blood rushing to the cut on her leg. There was no question that something was after her, two of them actually. Had Benjamin created a house of poltergeists with his final acts as the children's guardian? It didn't matter. Nothing did if she couldn't escape their wrath. Throwing all her weight against the basement door, Callie was sure she'd be free within seconds. The searing pain didn't deter her, yet the door stayed firmly in place. Shoving her body against it a second time, Callie felt herself starting to panic.

The attacks hadn't happened in years, yet she now felt the familiar grips of an anxiety ambush. Her chest constricted as her vision started to blur. The rapidly dimming light seemed to expedite the process as she lunged for the door one last time. The eerie sound from the other side had stopped just short of the basement steps. In a final act of desperation, Callie called out to the other side, pleading with God that it might be someone who could help her.

No savior or rescue team appeared, though, as she sank down on the small, rickety platform. The light flickered a warning. It wasn't going to last much longer. Closing her eyes, she started to sob, whispering a prayer while banging on the door. One flicker. Two. Three. The bulb hissed, becoming unreasonably bright for a split second before popping and enveloping her in darkness. With her sight now gone, her other senses became more acute, though it only made matters worse. The bottom step creaked. Not as it had when the weight of an adult stood on it but softer.

When the next step offered the same ominous sound, a renewed panic filled Callie. She could barely breathe. She grabbed her throat, her intentions unknown to even herself as she silently pleaded for air. Callie rapped her knuckles against the door as she sobbed, praying someone would hear her. The only sound that came from the other side was the return of the strange stepping and dragging. Benjamin. His spirit had to be out there, waiting for his ghost children to finish the job and restore Grant Manor back to its rightful owner—him.

Dead or alive, Callie knew Benjamin wanted them gone. Except for the bottom few steps, none of the others waned under her weight on the way down. When she felt a soft wisp of air against her cheek, the fear inside her turned back to panic. It was warm, moist, as one would expect when someone stood too close and breathed. The sudden proximity of the evil ghosts renewed her sense of urgency. Banging on the door again, Callie dragged herself back to her feet and violently shoved against the door, wiggling the handle as she tried fruitlessly to free herself and prolong her life.

"What do you want from me?" she screamed.

Her question was met with silence, save for the faint giggling of the children. Callie sobbed, remembering her own beautiful little girl playing happily outside with her husband. Unwilling to give in, she started to pray again as she worked the handle, the eerie laughter growing closer with each passing second. She crumbled into a ball, overwhelmed by the events as she continued to slam her fist into the door. Time lost all meaning. The spirits seemed content to torment her as seconds turned into minutes. Callie had resigned herself to her fate, not knowing if she'd been trapped for a few minutes or a few hours when a new sound emerged from the other side.

It was a familiar voice that filled her heart again with hope as she violently pounded on the door and screamed for Mike. His telltale footsteps came at a rapid pace as he jerked open the door. Callie tumbled out, not yet on her feet, as he lifted her from the ground. The fear and concern in his eyes were more than she could handle as she held him close, Lizzy looking on in shocked horror at the sight of her bloodied and disheveled mother. Mike gingerly lifted Callie into his arms and carried her to the kitchen, setting her on the island counter as one might a wounded child or animal. He barked out orders to Lizzy as Callie slowly started to regain her composure.

"What the hell happened?" Mike demanded. "Look at you. You're a bloody mess! Did you try to get the ornaments cleaned up? Sweetheart, I told you I would help you with that."

She shook her head. "No…"

"Did you trip? Dang," he gave a low whistle. "That's a nasty cut on your leg. Lizzy, grab the first aid kit. Look at us. Neither of us can make it a day without getting hurt around here."

Mike chuckled. Callie knew he was trying his best to lighten the mood, given how shaken she was. All she could do was sit there, too stunned to talk or tell Mike about what she'd just endured. Callie had almost forgotten about the slice Mike had acquired the day before, thanks to the old house. Now she knew it wasn't just a string of bad luck, though. There was something dark and sinister about the house. It had an evil inside it that no human would be able to overpower.

"What happened, sweetheart?" Mike asked again, his voice low and soothing.

"It was the children," she whispered.

His brow arched. "Children? You mean child? Like Lizzy? Did she lock the door by mistake?"

"No, Mike. The children, Vera and Mar—"

"Here, Daddy!" Lizzy beamed as she reappeared. "Mommy, are you going to be okay?"

Callie swallowed. She couldn't talk to Mike with Lizzy around. It would just scare the poor girl. Instead, she plastered a smile on her face and nodded, promising her daughter everything was going to be okay. Mike saw the lie behind her words and frowned but said nothing. There would be plenty of time for them to talk later. All Callie wanted to do was get out of the manor and as far away from it as possible. There was no way in hell she was going to let the ghost children claim her family, not even for a free mansion.

13

"*J*esus, what happened?" Mike asked, his voice laced with concern.

Callie shook her head. "I…I don't know anymore. Mike, I don't think I was alone down there."

He stiffened. "You think someone is in the house? I'll be right back."

She grabbed his arm. "No, not like that."

"What are you talking about? You just said—"

"I know what I said," Callie hissed. "I didn't mean a person."

Mike sighed, visibly relaxing some. The house was old and had its quirks. It was no surprise to him that Callie would make it out to be more than it really was. She'd been on a ghost kick ever since she and Lizzy had found the old cemetery. Mike had already made a point of asking Frank to put a lock on the gate, though he didn't tell his wife. If she managed to venture back there, he'd tell her it was for Lizzy's safety. Granted, he doubted she

78

was going to return to the family plot. She'd been shaken ever since discovering it.

"Callie..." he started.

"Don't patronize me or take that tone with me, Mike. I'm not crazy. I know there was something down there with me."

"Easy now. I'm not saying you're wrong. I just think maybe a mouse or bird might have gotten in and spooked you."

"Do mice lock doors and blow out lights?" Callie snapped.

His jaw twitched. He'd been married to Callie long enough to know when she wasn't going to hear reason. Whatever had spooked her was still fresh in her mind. He went back to cleaning the cut on her calf. It wasn't deep, but the flesh wound had bled a good bit. Gingerly, he put an antibacterial ointment on it before carefully topping it off with a bandage. When he was done with her leg, he took her hand in his. Three of the four knuckles had been busted open when she'd tried to get out. It was going to leave some nasty scabs and bruising, but otherwise, the damage seemed superficial.

"I don't know what to say," he muttered. "I think we need to get an electrician out here to take a look at things."

"And the door? How do you explain it being locked? Did a wayward bird do that, too?"

"All of these doors have the original skeleton keys in them. A gust of wind—"

"Jesus, really?"

79

"Well, sorry for trying to find a reasonable explanation instead of hopping right on the 'haunted house' train."

"Mike—"

"No," he snapped. "I'm not going to have this argument with you again. This is our home now. Once we get everything checked out, things will be easier. Why can't you just admit that you might have been a little scared down there in the dark? People's minds play tricks on them all the time, you know."

"So that's what you think this is? You think that I just made this shit up? I must have accidentally locked myself in the basement, blown out both lights, and done all that just to get you to move?"

"There," he growled. "Right there, you just said it yourself. You want to move; you hate it here. It doesn't matter that we can make this place our home or that Lizzy and I are happy. You just see a decrepit old mansion that's too much work."

"Is that really what you think? Why would I agree to move out here and let you get a loan—"

"Let me?" Mike hissed. "Now I get it."

"Mike, I didn't mean it like that," Callie muttered. "I'm sorry. I know you love this house."

He took her hands in his again, releasing a heavy sigh as he kissed her forehead. The tension started to melt away from his body. Callie was like a strong liquor to him. Her very presence seemed to calm him down. He knew he'd flown off the handle at her when it was apparent she was still shaken from the incident. Who could blame her?

For a superstitious woman, being trapped in a creepy basement had to mess with her mind. They couldn't leave Grant Manor. Even if one of her fictional ghosts came to life at that second and decided to have a conversation with the duo. He'd already accepted the loan and started buying materials.

"I didn't mean to dismiss your feelings," Mike said after a pause. "If you really feel like this house has something more than just bad electrical and plumbing, we can look into it. I'm sure this town has a priest or pastor, someone who can come give it a good exorcism."

Callie grinned. "Why do I get the feeling there's a little sarcasm in your voice?"

He laughed and shrugged. "Honey, I just want you to be happy here, and I know you're not. If you want someone to come out here to handle your ghosts, we'll make it happen."

"They aren't *my* ghosts. I'm pretty sure it was the little kids that Benjamin—"

Suddenly, things were starting to come together for Mike. Callie had always been over-protective of Lizzy. She was an only child, and both parents loved to dote on her. Knowing Callie thought the ghost of the children murdered there were still lingering made sense. She saw Benjamin's parenting failures as a warning sign. The only thing he could do was make sure Callie was content. The last thing they needed was her running around, telling prospective guests that the house and its ghosts were trying to kill her.

"All right then, the ghost children. We'll get a priest in here."

She shook her head. "No, you're right. It's probably just my imagination. Why don't we get the repair crew in here, then we can see what happens after that?"

"Are you sure? I don't mind making a big donation to whatever church they've got in this little town to put your mind at ease."

"I don't think that's going to cut it," she muttered. "Listen, I don't know what happened to me down there, but I know what I saw. Those two are still here; they want us gone. They don't want us in the house."

"Well, that's too bad for them because this is our home now, right? We've got the deed fair and square. If they want to stick around, they can follow the same rules as the living children, which means no locking Mom in the basement anymore."

"You're patronizing me again," she grumbled.

Mike laughed and pulled her into his arms. "I am, just a little, though. What do you want me to do here, Callie? If you don't want to get help, then it must not be that big of a deal, right?"

"I just don't know anymore. I wish it was all in my head, but I don't think that it is."

"Maybe you should go talk to someone. This has been a ton of change for all of us."

"You want me to go see a shrink?" she asked.

He shrugged. "Why not? You've made me go a couple times when I was starting to get really depressed. It might do you some good. This has been a lot of change for everyone."

"Living in a haunted house isn't the same as having writer's block," she snapped.

He sighed and set about putting away the first aid kit. Lizzy had disappeared back into her room the second she had found out her mother was going to be okay. It didn't seem like any answer Mike gave his wife was going to ease her mind. Marriage was a wonderful blessing, but sometimes he wished she'd have a little more faith in his decision-making and a little less in her pretend God.

"What can I do here?" he asked, feeling defeated.

She shook her head. "I don't know. I guess there's nothing we can do, right? Let's get the repair crew in here like you said. Maybe once everything is fixed and running smoothly, you'll finally believe me."

"It's not that I don't believe you...I just want to rule out everything else first."

"Including the possibility that I might be insane?" she asked.

He cringed. "Now, I didn't say that. I thought—"

"Yeah," she snapped. "That's the problem. You thought you knew what was best like you always do, and I'm just the crazy Catholic you married!"

Callie jumped down off the island and stormed out of the kitchen. Mike knew better than to follow her as he watched her slip out the front door and set off in the direction of the woods. Things would get better; he knew it. He hoped the good times would come soon, though. They had everything riding on the success of the manor.

Walking away now would surely cripple not just their finances but their relationship as well. Mike's heart fluttered. He couldn't imagine a life without Callie, but now, he couldn't imagine it without Grant Manor, either. Hopefully, that wouldn't be a decision he'd have to make.

14

"You continue to amaze me, woman," Mike said affectionately. "I can't believe what you've managed to do with this place in just a few days. How are you feeling?"

"Okay, not bad," she admitted. "There doesn't seem to be an infection, thank God. I don't think I want to go get a tetanus shot thanks to a rusty nail."

"Well, that bastard nail won't be giving you any more problems."

Callie burrowed deeper into his arm, her cheeks hot with embarrassment though his statement was well warranted. The couple looked around the manor. Everything on the first floor had been dusted, cleaned, swept, or washed. Not a single box was still packed save for the surviving ornaments Mike had put up the day before. Callie had been perfectly happy with letting him do the cleanup in the basement after her accident two days prior. Now, the house was finally starting to look like a home.

The towering windows and newly laundered curtains filled the house with bright rays of sunlight.

She could be in any room of the house and simply look outside to check on Lizzy, a fact that Callie greatly appreciated. They'd sat down the young girl and given her very specific boundaries for playing outside, but it didn't stop Callie from having a little trepidation about Lizzy's newfound sense of adventure. Thankfully, their daughter hadn't brought up her imaginary friend again since leaving the cemetery. While her curiosity was piqued by the disappearance of the "friend," Callie didn't push or question Lizzy about it, deciding instead to let a good thing go unprovoked.

Outside, the couple heard the telltale sounds of a vehicle bumbling up the driveway. Mike grinned at Callie, and she smiled back. They were both excited about the new arrivals but for very different reasons. Callie had set up the appointment with the electricians and was looking forward to getting to know a few locals. She had every intention of making them feel welcome and at ease in the massive manor. Mike was simply excited to have work being started on the property. He'd done what he could, but his tradesman skills were limited at best. Unless it consisted of housework or the bare basics like painting, he was outside his comfort zone.

"There they are," Mike said.

"Should I offer them something to drink?" Callie asked. "I'm going to make some sweet tea. I don't know anyone who wouldn't want a glass on a hot day like this. Do you think they've been here before?"

He chuckled. "I don't know, sweetheart, but I bet you can ask them when they get out. You said they were the only company in town, right?"

Callie nodded. "The only licensed electricians. I got a few numbers from the little hardware store of guys who are electricians but not licensed. I figured this way, if the place goes up in flames, at least our rears will be covered."

"Are you hoping it goes up in flames?" Mike asked.

She shrugged. "Honestly, I don't know anymore. If you'd have asked me that two days ago, I'd have lit the match myself. It's amazing what a little elbow grease can do, though."

"See, honey, I told you it just needed a little love. No more ghosts, right?"

"Right," she mumbled.

Callie wasn't as sure as her husband. Things had been going so well, though, that she couldn't bring herself to tell him that the house still gave her the creeps. The sensation of being watched was almost constant now, no matter what Callie was doing. Thankfully, whatever angry spirits were lingering seemed to avoid Mike. It was bringing the couple back together again. She wanted to be with her husband any time it was possible. The couple made their way to the front porch and watched the white van pull up. After several minutes, Callie started to get nervous.

"Why aren't they getting out?" she asked.

Mike sighed and shook his head. "I don't know. I'm going to go talk to them. Maybe they aren't sure they're at the right place."

"How many other houses have you seen on this road?" Callie asked.

Mike grinned, rolling his eyes. He knew just as well as she did that Grant Manor was the only property on the three-mile strip. As he approached the van, the driver's side door opened, and a man in his late fifties emerged. He glared at the house, his gaze moving over Callie to where Mike was standing. Mike waved at the guy, but he didn't reciprocate. Instead, he jerked his head for the man in the passenger seat to get out. The other gentleman glared at his presumed boss but slowly climbed out to stand next to him. Mike closed the distance, his hand outstretched as he smiled.

The man looked at Mike's hand before taking it, though he seemed to ponder letting Mike dangle without the shake. Instantly, Mike noted how unhappy the older man seemed to be there. The other electrician was closer to Mike's age, though he didn't seem any more thrilled about being at Grant Manor. Mike clenched his jaw. He was determined to make the best of the situation. It was common knowledge what had happened to Benjamin and his wards. He and Callie had expected some level of hostility from the townspeople over being related to the murderous old man.

"Mike Grant," he said. "It's a pleasure to meet you. I sure am grateful you fellas were able to make it out here so fast. We've had a heck of a time with the electrical."

"I'm sure," the elderly man grumbled. "Conner, this is my boy, Philip. Your old lady said you needed a consultation."

"Sure do. I would love to give you guys all the work for the place right away. I just want to make sure I've got enough to cover it!" Mike joked.

Neither man laughed as a stagnant silence filled the air. Mike heard Callie approaching from behind and eased some. She was much better with people than he was. When she reached them, her bubbly personality started right away as she enthusiastically told the pair how excited they were to have them there. Still, the air of unease persisted. After a few more minutes of Callie asking them questions about the community, silence fell again. Taking the opportunity to get the ball rolling, Mike started for the house. He didn't notice that only one of the men followed after him.

Callie shifted uneasily. "Would you like some tea? It's fresh and sweet."

The man shook his head.

"Are you sure? We really appreciate you guys getting out here so fast. This old place needs all the help it can get."

"No, thank you."

She pursed her lips. "Okay then, why don't you come inside? The sun sure is warm today. You've got to be melting standing out here. I can't imagine with those long sleeves—"

"No, I'm fine."

"Really? It's so hot! Maybe just the porch?"

"Listen, lady. I appreciate you giving my family the business for this place, but if it's all the same to you, I'd just as soon not come near Grant Manor."

"Oh? Why's that? Don't tell me you believe all those gossips in town. Mr. Grant lost his mind; it was a tragic thing that happened here, but now we're trying to make it a place for everyone to enjoy."

He snorted. "You can do or say whatever you want, but that house has haunted this town for generations. You're lucky my pops even came out here. I tried to talk him out of it."

"It sounds like your father is a reasonable man then," Callie snapped. "If you aren't going to work, why are you even here?"

He glared at her. "To make sure my father makes it back out of this place alive."

"Oh please, that's ridiculous. What do you think is going to happen? My husband and I are going to push him down the steps, maybe then blame it on the house? This is just silly."

He shrugged. "I don't really care what your opinion is. I know this property. I was here two years ago when the electrical started shorting out in the basement. Now, you can't tell me this place is normal."

Callie's stomach lurched. "You know, it's funny you mention the basement. That's exactly where we're having problems this time around. Maybe your superstation was just bad workmanship. I'd like a copy of the original work you did to the basement if you don't mine."

"Sure thing, you can call my mom at the office and get everything you want, but I'd recommend finding yourself another electrician because I'm not going to let my father come over here and end up like old Benj—"

"Philip!" came a booming voice.

Callie spun around to see the elderly man slowly making his way down the steps.

"Get me the four-tenths from the back," he grumbled. "And get your ass in here. I need another set of hands."

"Pops…"

"Don't argue with me now, boy."

Philip glared at Callie. Whatever he had going through his mind, it was apparent he disliked Callie as much as she did him.

15

"*H*e didn't even want to go in the house," Callie hissed. "I wish we could find someone else; we might just need to bring in an outsider."

Mike sighed. "Oh, I'm sure that will go over well. There are tons of men without work in this town and we want to bring in someone else."

"Well, it's not my fault none of the other electricians bothered to get bonded and insured. The only reason they are here is that they fixed the basement years ago to start with. I really doubt you'll get them to work on anything else."

"Are you sure you were reading the situation correctly?"

Callie glared at him.

Mike raised his hands in surrender.

"I guess it doesn't matter. You said they'd be back tomorrow to finish the job, right? After that, we can figure out if we want them to keep coming back," Callie muttered.

"Sweetheart, I think you're getting worked up over nothing. Everyone has a bad day or two. You probably just caught him on an off day. His father seemed perfectly friendly and helpful. Hell, he showed me where the breaker box was, so next time we blow a fuse or light, I won't get electrocuted."

"Did he also tell you he was the one who wired the basement two years ago? We are just paying him to fix a problem he created."

"He also showed me where mice had chewed through the wiring, honey. That's the only reason things were flickering down there when you were stuck. It wasn't his fault, nor was it Casper, okay? Just a few field mice who saw an empty house and wanted to move in. I've already set traps for them."

Callie cringed. She hated the idea of killing innocent animals, even if they were a bit of a nuisance. Still, getting rid of them was better than the thought of having to go back down into the basement and relive what had happened to her days prior. She couldn't bring herself to push the issue with Mike. It was apparent he was already on edge since the electricians had left. Though the afternoon had cooled enough for them to enjoy their lunch on the front porch, Mike was still tense about the rest of the day. They'd had the plumber, the second of three called, cancel on them at the last minute. Now they were waiting on the new company to show up.

"They're half an hour late," Mike grumbled.

"I'm sure they will be here. Not everyone in this town can hate this house, right?"

"I don't know. It's starting to look that way...."

Before he could complain any more, an old blue pick-up came barreling down the driveway. With each bump it hit, the contents of the bed became suspended briefly in the air. The stickers on the side indicated it was the plumber they'd been waiting on. When a friendly looking man with dirty-blond hair emerged in overalls, Callie frowned. He hadn't been what she was expecting, though one look at Mike told her the new plumber would do just fine. He always seemed to latch on to those unique individuals. With a toothless grin, the man jogged up the steps and cheerfully introduced himself. Callie wondered if "unique" was an understatement in describing the man.

"Name's Gavin McCoy. You must be Mike and Callie! Sure is a pleasure to meet you both! Boy, you got one heck of a sweet deal on this place, huh? I can't wait to get back inside and take a peek!"

"Back inside?" Callie pressed. "You've been here before?"

"I'm not surprised. It seems like everyone has something to say about Grant Manor," Mike muttered.

Gavin burst into laughter, slapping his knee as his face turned red. He reminded Callie of someone, but she couldn't quite place him. She couldn't tell if the man was insane or just enthusiastic about his work, but either way, he would do the job, and that was all that mattered at that point. She and Lizzy were both tired of taking cold baths with water the color of weak coffee. For all she cared, he could have eight eyeballs and speak only in riddles and she'd still let him work on the damn house.

"Well now, don't you worry about what people have to say. They're full of old spite for this place and the fella who owned it. Now personally, I don't care what happened here before. I reckon you folks are just about tired of hearing the stories."

"Stories?" Callie pressed.

"Callie," Mike warned. "We are happy to have you, Gavin. Why don't I show you where—well, never mind, you mentioned you've been here before?"

He nodded. "Sure have, more times than I can count. Frank is getting up there in age. Any time he needs a hand, he gives me a call. Awe, shucks, I suppose I should apologize for my timing, too. Me and the old man just got to gabbing, and one thing led to another. Before I knew it, I was running late and hauling tail to get over here."

It dawned on Callie that Gavin reminded her of Frank. The similarities in their personalities were almost identical now that she had made the connection. Still, Frank hadn't mentioned any kids of his living in the area. Nor had he ever mentioned a wife.

"Are you Frank's son?" Callie asked.

Gavin snorted. "No, ma'am, but I sure wish I was! My old man was nothing but a deadbeat drunk. Frank's the one who looked after me and my ma till she passed back in '98. He made sure I finished my education, and old Benjamin even let me stay here a spell and work for rent when I needed a hand years back."

"So, you knew Benjamin?" Mike asked.

"Well, of course! I bet not as well as you did, given you being his blood and all, but he was still a right fine man. Shame about what happened to him, a damn shame. People around here will give you hell for moving into this place but don't let it slow you down. The more you make this place all pretty like you're doing, the more they'll love ya for it."

"Wow, so you really do know the house. Any idea why the damn water heater isn't working?" Mike asked, forgoing the comment about his relationship with his grandfather.

"Ha! I told old Ben to replace that monster a year ago in the fall. Guess he never got around to it before...you know...." Gavin made a stabbing motion with his hand into his neck.

Callie cringed as Mike cleared his throat and stood. Despite his rough edges, there wasn't much to dislike about Gavin. As the two men disappeared into the house, Callie stood and followed them. She had no intention of going back into the basement if it could be helped, but the rest of the house felt fine. Plus, she was intrigued by Gavin. He seemed like the kind of man who enjoyed a conversation or two. Callie wanted answers about what the townsfolk really thought, and Gavin was the open book to give her those details.

She watched with intense concentration as Gavin talked about what he was doing. Mike was more than happy to run back and forth throughout the house with the baby monitor, shutting off sinks and appliances at Gavin's command as he talked with Callie about everything he did. Before long, she knew more about the stranger's upbringing than she did most of her extended family. He was relaxing to be around and friendly to boot. After twenty minutes of fiddling with things, Gavin let slip that he had a boyfriend in another town, and instantly, Callie invited him and his partner over for dinner.

The young man seemed genuinely touched by her gesture, agreeing to the meal later that night almost instantly. If nothing else, it gave her the time she'd need to pry him for more information. Plus, Callie had been on the lookout for a replacement for Frank ever since the day she'd met him. Who better to replace the aging groundskeeper than his self-proclaimed protégé? Within half an hour, she had hot water in her kitchen thanks to his backwoods rigging. After promising he'd be back for dinner later that night and have a new water heater in before the end of the week, the plumber left again in his pickup, though they could hear his country music blasting for several miles down the road.

16

"So, there he was, six and a half feet of delicious country charm, standing bare-assed in the middle of San Francisco! What could I do?" Sam asked. "I just had to take him home with me. Two years later, he talked me into making our long-distance relationship a real one, and we've been together ever since."

Callie smiled at the happy couple as they gazed lovingly at each other. She could see from the look in their eyes that they had a solid relationship. Never in a million years would Callie think she'd find the perfect couple defying odds in a small town laced with outdated, orthodox beliefs. It was refreshing to know she and Mike had made friends. Unfortunately, the same couldn't be said for the rest of the town. They all still seemed to enjoy hating the Grant family.

"This really is a beautiful home," Sam said. "I can't believe you've never brought me here before."

Gavin blushed and shrugged. "Frank was always really

weird about having people over to the main house, even after Ben bit the bullet...well...you know what I mean."

Mike chuckled and stood, grabbing another round of drinks for everyone as Callie listened to Gavin talk about the property and her husband's grandfather with obvious love. In the back of her mind, though, she noted Mike's absence, well aware that he'd have to go to the basement cellar for a fresh bottle of wine. It had given her the brief moment alone with Gavin that she needed. Thankfully, the conversation had already turned back to Grant Manor, making the transition into questions simple.

"So, you were close with Ben as well?" Callie asked Gavin. "Did you see any of the early signs that something was wrong? I hope you don't mind my asking. As a nurse, I have a bad habit of prying too much."

"Of course not! You've got as much right as anyone else to know about the history of this place. Course I didn't know until tonight that Mike and old Ben weren't close. I can't say I'm surprised, though, that he ended up with the place."

"Why do you say that?" Callie asked.

Gavin shrugged. "I knew he wasn't going to leave it to them kids he took on. Anyone with half a brain could tell you that. Not with the history of this place and what it does to the owners. He'd never bring that evil down on them."

"He murdered them," Callie reminded Gavin. "That doesn't sound like a loving caregiver. Even if he'd reached the stage of dementia."

"Oh no, he wasn't crazy. He had a mind like a steel trap, always did, right up to the end."

Her jaw dropped. "Again, he killed two kids. Are you really trying to say he did that while he was sane? I don't know if that makes things better or worse."

"He didn't kill them," Gavin muttered.

"Gavin…" Sam whispered. "Don't start that again."

"No," Callie stammered. "Please continue. What do you mean he didn't kill them?"

Gavin sighed. "It was this damn house…I can't believe you two didn't look into it more before loading up and moving down. Honestly, I was plum surprised to find out it was occupied again."

"Ah, so you think the house killed him, too?" Callie asked. "I've actually heard that one before, from Frank, I believe."

"Well, give that old fart more credit than you do. He'd know if something was off with Ben. Hell, he practically raised those two kids right along with the old man. He loved them like they were his own."

"I don't know," Callie muttered. "I love my daughter; I'd never hurt her."

"Neither did he. I tell you, it was the house that did it. I don't know how, but I saw him and the kids not even five hours before that awful incident. He hated this place but loved those children."

"If he hated this house so much, why didn't he sell it and take them somewhere else?"

Gavin grinned. "We could ask you the same thing."

"Well, because we can't, obviously. The way the will

was written, we're not allowed to," Callie gasped.

Gavin nodded in understanding. "That's right. You aren't the first round of Grants to move in. Hell, that line goes back so far that I think you can trace it to before the Civil War. This house has a way of getting people and hanging on to them. Granted, Ben and his family were the first Grants I met, but you should talk to Frank about it. He'll tell you this house has a history with your family."

Callie frowned. "I don't think Frank likes me very much."

"Don't take it too personally. Frank doesn't like anyone. Plus, how chipper would you be if everyone around you kept dying off? I know he thinks it's the house, too; you said as much. Are you sure you guys want to stay here?"

"My husband doesn't believe in silly superstitions like that," Callie replied.

"Yeah? Is that why you guys are still here? Because he thinks it's safe? What about you? How does it make you feel?" Gavin asked.

A chill ran through Callie despite the warm temperature outside. She couldn't meet her new friend's gaze. Deep down, Callie knew he was right. There was something wrong with the house, no matter how she tried to deny it. The lingering sensation of being watched stayed with her almost twenty-four hours a day despite Mike's having checked the entire house for unlatched windows or unlocked doors.

Nothing was getting in or out unless it moved through the solid walls, which was entirely unrealistic for Mike, a fact that still irked Callie. It wasn't like she was asking him to believe in unicorns, but some acknowledgment that the house was eerie would have been nice. Before she could reply, Mike appeared with a tray of fresh drinks. Callie did her best to dive into the conversation while steering it away from the many ghostly implications. He smiled and held up an empty ice bag.

"Looks like we are drinking the German way. One of our mice friends must have gotten ahold of it," Mike said.

Callie frowned. "In the freezer? I don't think mice can get in there, honey."

"I put it in the wine cellar, actually. It gets just as cold down there, and this way, we don't have to worry about it taking up freezer space. We can stock that bad boy up for the winter and not lose any space. Smart, right?" Mike asked.

Callie burst into laughter. "Smart. Although I'm not sure how much good the penny pinching did you. Don't worry, I think we can all survive with just the wine this time. Do you boys want to take this onto the porch? I need to go tuck Lizzy in—"

"I'll get her, honey. You look like you're having a great time. I'm happy you've made friends. Gentleman, I will see you in a little bit."

As they made their way to the front porch, Callie grabbed the discarded bag to drop into the can outside. If they had mice, she didn't want the smell of them attracting others. Gavin and Sam settled in on the porch, lost in their own little world of conversation while she walked to the other side of the driveway, opening the lid and tossing in the bag. Something about the clear plastic caught her attention. Before she let go, she pulled it back out again and slowly started to unfold it.

The tears in the bag weren't like anything she'd seen before and certainly not done by any small country mouse. It looked like the bag had been cut open deliberately, as if someone wanted it all to spill out and melt. The large gouges threw her off as she frowned. What purpose would it serve to slice open a bag of ice, and furthermore, who would want to do that? Making a mental note to ask Lizzy about it the next day, she made her way back to the couple just as the lights on the front porch started to flicker. Her stomach rolled, but Gavin was on his feet in a matter of seconds.

"Don't worry! I've got this. I know this place like the back of my hand. I'll see what's going on."

Sam whistled. "Isn't he something?"

Callie laughed and nodded. "He sure is. I think you've got yourself a keeper."

Gavin bowed with a dramatic flourish before disappearing. Callie thanked him and settled into a chair next to Sam, quickly losing herself in conversation. It wasn't until Mike appeared later that they realized Gavin hadn't returned yet. Callie's hair stood on end as they started to look for him, following the path he'd made around the exterior of the house to find the faulty wiring. The cellar door was open, beckoning to her as she climbed down the worn steps. The instant she cleared the foundation, she saw his body. Callie screamed as Gavin's body twitched. He was still alive.

17

"Mike!" Callie screamed. She ran to her fallen friend, nearly reaching him when arms wrapped around her waist. Callie fought against her husband.

"Dammit, Callie, wait!" he yelled, shoving her back toward the steps.

She stumbled backward, watching Mike dart to the opposite side of the basement to the breaker box. Ten seconds later, the basement went dark, but Gavin stopped twitching. It was then that Callie noticed the pool of water surrounding the young man. The instant the electrical current stopped coursing through his body, she was at his side. He was still breathing, though it was low and ragged. Rolling him onto his back, Callie elevated his head. In the back of her mind, she heard Mike calling for an ambulance.

"Oh my God," Sam stammered, collapsing onto the

ground next to his lover. "What happened? Gavin? Gavin, talk to me, please!"

"He's okay," Callie promised. "He will be, at least. He's still breathing."

"Why isn't he conscious then?" Sam asked.

"He just had one hell of current run through his body," Callie replied. "If he weren't breathing, then I'd be worried, but right now, his body is protecting him from the shock and pain. Mike, go get my smelling salts from the first aid bag."

He was up the steps and back down in a matter of seconds. Callie and Sam were already moving Gavin up the basement steps and into the damp grass. It didn't matter at that moment how it had happened. Callie had shifted into "nurse mode," her only concern was now the man lying in front of her. To the small town's credit, she heard the squad approaching just minutes after Mike had called. By the time they arrived, Gavin was sitting up. Callie snatched the oxygen mask from the medic, slipping it over Gavin's head as they loaded him onto a stretcher.

To Sam's credit, he kept his composure. Once again, Callie was baffled by the amount of love between the two men. The pair was loaded into the ambulance after Mike promised Gavin for a third time that he didn't ruin the evening with his medical emergency. The couple watched their new friends disappear down the driveway, the bright lights flashing against the black night. Wrapping his arm around his wife, Mike could feel Callie trembling still from the ordeal.

"What the hell happened?" Mike asked.

She shook her head. "I don't know. He went to see why the porch light shorted out."

"Come on," he grumbled.

Callie followed him back down into the basement. It smelled like burning plastic and vomit, a natural side effect of electrocution. A body always tried to save itself, even if the person wasn't conscious. It was pure luck that Gavin had collapsed first on his side before rolling over. Otherwise, they might not have made it in time. He would have drowned in his own puke. Callie's stomach rolled as Mike picked up the wires and inspected them. Instantly, she could see the confusion on his face.

"What's wrong?" she asked.

He shook his head. "I was down here not even three minutes ago, and this wire wasn't down."

"It's frayed, though. Do you think the mice got to it?"

"What mice?" he prompted. "I haven't seen a single one since we moved out here. You said there were a couple down here, but with all the commotion of us moving in, they should have cleared out by now. Not only that, but this looks like it was snapped, not chewed."

"Snapped?"

"Yeah," he muttered. "Like someone grabbed it and just pulled it apart."

"It's an electrical wire; I didn't think you could do that."

"You shouldn't be able to, at least not with newer houses, but the lines around here are so brittle, even Lizzy could pull some of them apart. Hell, yesterday I was up in the attic and stepped on a conductor, and it shattered."

"Then maybe it just gave way," Callie offered.

He shook his head again. "I don't know anymore. Maybe it was an accident but then why didn't I see it earlier?"

"It's been a long night; we've been drinking. I hope you aren't beating yourself up over this. It could have happened to anyone."

Mike frowned but nodded. Callie could tell he still didn't believe her. She didn't want to think about what the other explanations could be. She glanced around the dark basement. It still felt like someone was watching them. The children. A chill moved through her. Outside, someone started to pound on the cellar door, making Callie and Mike both jump as a dark figure loomed above. Her heart started to race until Frank appeared. She let out the breath she'd been holding, leaning into her husband's chest again for support.

"Everyone okay?" Frank asked, his voice laced with the fog that came from a deep slumber. "I saw the lights."

"Yeah...well no, not really. Gavin got electrocuted. He's going to be all right, but they took him to the hospital in Jackson just to be sure."

Frank went pale. "Gavin? *My* Gavin? What in the hell was he doing here?"

Callie cringed. "He came over for dinner, him and Sam. The lights on the porch shorted out, and he came to look—"

"Jesus, this fucking house is going to take everyone I love," Frank snapped. "I thought you people got an electrician out here! Gavin doesn't need to be running around this place. If you want to kill off your own kind, that's one thing—"

"Hey!" Mike's booming voice filled the air. "You better watch what you say to my wife."

Frank's jaw clenched. "I'm sorry, really. I am. I just–I don't know what came over me. You surprised me; I didn't know he was here. I thought I taught him better than to go running around, looking for hot wires in the dark."

"It wasn't his fault," Callie whispered. "It wasn't anyone's fault, a freak accident. The ice melted…we didn't know."

"Ice goes in the freezer," Frank growled.

Mike chuckled. "Yeah, thanks for that. Hey, man, he's going to be okay."

Frank nodded but said nothing. It was obvious he was still deeply shaken by the incident. After a few more apologies from the old guy, he headed back in the direction of his cabin beyond the tree line. Mike and Callie followed him out into the yard, watching him disappear down the trail. She couldn't shake the feeling that something was still wrong. Why did Frank blame them for what had happened?

"I just wanted to make some new friends," she sobbed. "I never meant for him to get hurt. What if he never forgives us?"

"Hey, now, sweetheart, this wasn't your fault, either, okay? That kid seems to love this old place; I don't think a little shock will keep him away. Gavin is going to be fine. You said it yourself, right? It's been a long night. I'm going to get the power back on, then I'll draw you a bath. How does that sound?"

"Really good," Callie admitted. "I'm going to go check on Lizzy."

"Okay, she was just about to fall asleep when I left. It seems she and her imaginary friend really wore themselves out today," Mike said as he kissed her forehead. "I'll be up in a few minutes."

"Ugh, stupid imaginary friends. I was hoping we were done with all that. I don't like it. You know that she said he's in the cemetery? His name is Mar—"

"Let it go, Callie," he firmly said. "We don't need to be starting this argument again right now. She's a kid. She saw the boy's name and decided she liked it for her friend. Stop reading into it so much."

"I wish I could believe that it's just her imagination."

"No," Mike snapped. "You just expect me to believe that it's a fucking ghost running around."

"Mike...I didn't mean it like that," Callie stammered, shocked by his anger.

"Let's just drop it for tonight."

Callie nodded, kissing his cheek before making her way back inside the house. Grabbing the wine glasses and bottles along the way, it felt eerie to be in the dark house. How Lizzy had slept through everything was baffling to her. Using her phone's flashlight to guide the way, she peeked into her daughter's room. The little girl was snoring softly, just like her father did. A smile crept across Callie's face as she leaned on the jamb, watching her daughter sleep. Outside, she caught a glimpse of Frank moving toward his house. His erratic movements snatched her attention.

The path he'd taken wasn't the one he'd shown Lizzy and her a few days prior. Instead, it moved along the lake, giving him a clear view of Grant Manor. Trepidation crept through her body as she shuddered. Mike was right; it had been a long and stressful ending to the evening. Tomorrow she would ask Frank about the trail. Just as Callie turned to leave the bedroom, she stole one final glance at Frank's retreating figure along the edge of the lake. Her heart pounded as she gasped. Two small shadows were following him as he walked.

18

*A*fter the events of the night before, Callie woke up feeling worn down. The start of a migraine threatened her plans for the afternoon. Several cups of coffee and a couple aspirin later, she managed to drag herself into the shower. She emerged refreshed just as Lizzy started to stir in her bedroom. Mike had left hours before, determined to repair the wires on his own.

Moving through the house, she checked the front door before making Lizzy a bowl of cereal. When the child was settled, Callie quietly slipped into the parlor to call Mike back. He'd tried to ring her twice, but the usual morning chaos had only just died down. Taking in the scenery, Callie couldn't help but stare at the groundskeeper's cabin. A chill tickled her spine. Frank was an eccentric man, to say the least.

"Hey, sweetheart," Callie said. "Are you finding what you need in Jackson?"

Mike sighed on the other end of the phone. "Yes and

no. I found the hardware and wiring I need, but I just got a call from the electricians."

"Uh oh, did you make a pointless trip? Are they coming out to fix it?"

"No, just the opposite, actually. They're refusing to set foot on the property again, even to get their check for last time."

"Damn," Callie muttered. "Let me guess, more small-town superstition?"

"Something like that. They heard about what happened last night."

She groaned. "Oh, for Christ's sake. Are you serious? Jesus, do they think we did it?"

"No, the opposite, actually. They are convinced we didn't. They think we should leave and light a match on the way out."

"So, it's the house again? They think the house is trying to kill people? Mike…maybe it's time we consider our options."

"Like what? Move back to the city so you can work seventy hours a week and I can be a failed writer? Because that's what you're pushing for."

"You aren't a failed writer…."

"No? How many books have I sold? Zero. I'm a failure as a writer. Jesus, just please back off, okay? Don't you see this is just making things worse? I need us to be a team. I need you, Callie. I need you to support me."

Callie cringed. She loved her husband despite his short fuse. He could be one of the kindest men, lovers, and fathers when he wasn't stressed or overwhelmed. Grant

Manor was bringing out the worst in him. Callie knew he was under a tremendous amount of pressure. If he'd just acknowledge there was something wrong with the manor, they could move on with their lives.

He wouldn't stop, though. He wouldn't give up until the bitter end, and Callie knew it. Mike was a fighter and a dreamer. She'd known him long before they were married. As the saying went, you couldn't teach an old dog new tricks, and Mike was the stubborn leader of their little pack. Hell would freeze over before he conceded defeat. It wouldn't do Callie any good to argue with him, at least not while he was so obviously worked up. Plus, she wasn't a fan of fighting over the phone. Some things just needed to be handled in person.

"I'm sorry, Mike. I know this is stressing you out. Why don't we talk about it when you get home?"

"Fine," he grumbled. "I don't know when that's going to be, though. I need to go find a freaking electrician now. Hopefully, that stupid town sees me dropping dimes on non-locals and they get their shit together. We'll probably have to find a new plumber to boot."

"No, we won't. Gavin texted me this morning after he got released from the hospital. They're on their way to pick up the truck they left last night, and he mentioned starting work on a few things. He's a good seed, sweet-heart. He wants to work for us and be here."

"Thank God, at least someone in this hell-hole knows a good opportunity when they see it."

"I think the locals are just being cautious," Callie mumbled.

He sighed. "I know, it just pisses me off. I'm willing to throw money at those people, and they're letting old superstitions get in the way."

"To be fair, Gavin was hurt here last night, and we still don't know why."

"Let's not get into that again. I'll be home as soon as I can, maybe even with a real electrician who won't shake in his work boots and clutch his cross every time he walks in."

Callie chuckled. "Good luck."

"I love you; you know that, right?" he asked.

"Forever and ever, my love."

She ended the call and stood, peeking into the kitchen to check on Lizzy. When the child saw her mother, she smiled and waved. Obviously done with her breakfast, Lizzy was ready to spend the afternoon exploring more of the property with her mom. For the first time since Callie had graduated college, she had downtime to sit around and do nothing. Though the journals Benjamin had left behind called to her, Lizzy would always be significantly more important than any mystery Callie might uncover between the pages of the notebooks. Before long, Lizzy was dressed and ready to start an adventure.

She pleaded with Callie to hurry as her mother folded and put away the last of the girl's laundry. Callie couldn't help but share in her daughter's excitement as they raced down the steps to the front door. When they reached the bottom, Callie skidded to a stop before nearly colliding with Frank. Her stomach lurched as her eyes moved past him to the front door. It had been locked just moments before. Immediately, she felt uneasy as his gaze moved from her to her daughter and back again.

"Lizzy, you can go ahead. I'll be out in a minute but stay away from the woods until I get there," she growled.

Her eyes never left Frank's though their icy blue sent a chill up her arms. When the girl was gone, she continued in a low, menacing tone. "How the hell did you get in here?" she demanded. "If you have a key, I want it right now. Do you hear me?"

"Easy now, no key. The door was standing wide open. Miss, I'd never just walk into someone's house—"

"Really? Because you just did, again," Callie snapped. "As a matter of fact, you seem to be making a habit of it."

"I told you that door's always been open every time I come round."

Callie noted the shocked look in his eyes. He seemed to be telling the truth, though anymore she found herself doubting her gut. It had never led her astray until they'd moved into Grant Manor. Now everything was throwing her off. Once again, she decided to give him the benefit of the doubt but made a mental note to have Mike pick up new locks for all of the doors, just as a little extra security. If Frank were telling the truth, he'd never notice the upgrade.

"What do you want?"

"I thought I'd come to get little Gavin's pickup for him. No use in him hauling himself all the way back out here—"

"He already spoke with us," Callie interrupted. "He's

coming out to get his truck and start on the plumbing. We aren't going to turn away a hard worker like him."

Frank paled. "He's going to be working for you?"

"Yes, and we're happy to have him. Plus, he might decide to take over the groundskeeper position when you retire."

"I don't like him working out here."

Callie gritted her teeth, fighting the snippy comment that came to mind. "What's your problem with him working here? It's good enough for you, me, and my husband, right?"

"You don't know what you're getting yourself into. This house is no place for him. I'd just as soon ask you to leave him be."

"Well, that's your opinion but not his or ours. If he wants to work here, we'll gladly take all the help we can get."

Frank's face turned bright red as he glared at her, spinning around on his heels and storming out of the house without another word. The entire interaction left Callie feeling uneasy. She quickly shot a text to Mike, asking him to grab new deadbolts for the doors. Snatching her keys and water bottle, Callie locked the door behind her and checked it twice to be safe before setting off after Lizzy. Her daughter was already down by the lake, making friends with every fish, frog, and duck that would come within fifteen feet of her.

They lingered by the water for a few more minutes before Lizzy grew bored with the wildlife. As they turned for the woods, Callie felt the familiar sensation of being watched again. She quickly scanned the horizon and felt her cheeks flush. Frank was staring at them from his cabin porch, and while she couldn't make out his features, she could almost feel the hatred that seemed to ooze from his gaze.

19

"He gives me the creeps," Callie whispered. "The way that his face fell when I said Gavin was going to be working here, you'd think I just gave the kid a death sentence! Not to mention the way he watches Lizzy and me. I just wish he'd take his damn retirement and leave."

"I know, sweetheart. He has to be pushing sixty, though. He can't stay on here forever. Has he actually said anything disparaging to you, or is it just a feeling?"

Callie glared at Mike when he put finger quotes around the word "feeling." His complete lack of belief in intuition, the supernatural, and gut instinct was downright infuriating at times. Why was it so hard for him to believe in things he couldn't see? Still, she wasn't going to drop the subject like he obviously wanted her to. It was starting to become a problem. Callie handed Mike a flathead screwdriver as she watched him replace the lock on the kitchen door. The front, basement, and pantry doors were already done, setting her mind at ease a little.

Mike sighed and stood. "I'm sorry. I know how you feel about all this. I just think you're making a mountain out of a molehill. The old fart probably just feels threatened now that he knows Gavin is going to be working here. If we don't need him anymore, he's basically retired, whether he's ready for it or not."

"I guess," she muttered. "I'll be happy when he's done for good."

"Well, now that this is done," Mike said, pointing to the new locks, "I think you'll feel much better. If he had a key before that we didn't know about, it won't do him any good."

"Don't tell me you honestly believe the wind was unlocking and opening the doors."

"Of course not," Mike replied.

She didn't believe him but didn't press the issue. It was bad enough that he doubted the manor had a few more spirits than she'd have liked, but now Mike seemed to be in complete denial. Callie was starting to question how much of what was happening was real versus a side effect of sleep deprivation. Despite normally being a heavy sleeper, she'd woken at least a dozen times in the week they'd been at the manor. Sensing his wife's fatigue, Mike took her hand and led her upstairs to the bedroom. With Lizzy fast asleep and the doors now secured, all he wanted was his wife to be at ease. The single kiss he gave her when they reached their bed quickly turned into more until sated; they drifted off to sleep.

* * *

CALLIE WOKE WITH A START, the neon alarm alerting her to the late hour as Mike softly snored next to her. Slipping out of bed, she tugged on her robe and crept from the room, trying her best not to disturb him. He'd always been the type to wake at any noise. It often baffled her how she lacked the maternal instinct to wake when Lizzy was small and needed to be fed, yet Mike was often already at their daughter's bedside. Creeping down the main steps, she checked the front door again to make sure it was locked as she avoided the old floorboards that always wanted to groan beneath a human's weight. After the first few nights of restless sleep, she'd quickly learned which ones would wake the rest of the house along with her.

The kitchen was illuminated by a single solar night-light she kept on the windowsill. Late at night, it gave off an eerie glow, but it was still better than nothing at all. The steps she followed to bury the nightmares had become second nature. Grabbing a glass from the cabinet and the sleeping pills from the top of the pantry, she side-stepped around the closed cubby door. It didn't matter that Lizzy had been warned away from the crawlspace; it still gave Callie bad vibes. Her gaze stayed trained on the small door until she was back in the safety of the kitchen.

Popping open the bottle, Callie swallowed the white oval prescription. She chased it down with a swig of slightly off-colored water. Hopefully, the pipes would be running cleaner by the time Gavin finished his repairs, but for the time being, she knew there was nothing to be done about the well water. It would take a few minutes for the pill to kick in, but she had no desire to return to her bedroom. Despite the uneasy feeling the house gave her, it was still a unique experience to be in it alone after dark. She couldn't hear her husband or daughter's snoring from the main floor.

As a matter of fact, she realized she couldn't hear anything. A shudder raked her shoulders, though she tried to shrug it off as the same discomfort she'd felt from the very beginning of their lives at Grant Manor. This time, it felt different. The air almost had a thick quality to it, making her gasp despite the air-conditioning running at full force. Her lips pursed as she strained to listen. She couldn't hear the powerful motor running beneath her feet in the basement. Finishing the last of her water, Callie grabbed the bottle and tightened the lid before trekking back to the pantry.

Somewhere behind her in the kitchen, Callie heard movement, but she didn't dare turn around. All she could think about was what was in front of her. At that point, she'd given up on finding the culprit who lurked in her kitchen. Mike had made it clear that the mice would take some time to find a new home now that the manor had living occupants again. Plus, she was facing a much more terrifying reality. Her eyes moved to the cubby as the color drained from her face. She couldn't breathe whatsoever anymore; her throat felt dry. The bottle tumbled from her grip, rolling across the uneven floor to the small, open door.

"Momma? Is that you?" Came Lizzy's voice.

Callie nearly toppled over with relief as she knelt down to retrieve the wayward bottle. "Lizzy! What are you doing in there again? You are in big trouble, little lady; this isn't a good place for you to be playing. Plus, it's way past your bedtime!"

"Momma, I don't want to go swimming in the lake."

She chuckled, grabbing the bottle and setting it back onto the counter before returning to the cubby and slumping down on the floor next to it. Her heart was finally beating at a normal place again.

"Honey, what on earth are you talking about? We don't have to go swimming anywhere. We only taught you how to swim so early so you could if you ever needed—"

"The water is too dark, Momma. Somethings wrong with it. There shouldn't be so much mud."

"Do you think maybe we can talk about this tomorrow? It's late; you need to get back to bed. Do you want me to make you a cup of hot chocolate? It will have to be our little secret, though. I don't think Daddy would be very happy if he found out you were in there again."

"I don't like it here, Momma. It's dark and cold. I want to be with you."

Callie smiled and crawled to the cubby door. "Then get out here silly—"

She reached into the small space, feeling around for Lizzy in the dark. When she couldn't reach her, Callie leaned down to get a better idea of where her daughter had managed to wedge herself. The color drained from her face. Every nerve in her body was yelling for her to run, but she couldn't move. Something was wrong with her daughter. The worn nightgown she had on wasn't one Callie had bought for her. As the little girl turned to face her mother, Callie screamed. Blood coated the front of the nightgown, a gaping wound in her throat gushed an inhuman amount of blood as the creature spoke.

"Momma? You're supposed to be in the lake...with the others."

20

---

*C*allie woke to Mike shaking her, her body drenched with sweat. The bloodied image of the little girl still playing through her mind. She could smell the iron in the blood. It was enough to make her roll over and puke up the evening's dinner in the trash can next to the bed, with Mike barely moving in time. He was talking to her, his voice laced with concern, but the disorientation prevented her from answers. It was almost impossible for her to comprehend what he was saying. Glancing at the clock, she realized only two minutes had passed since the last time she woke.

"Sweetheart, hey! Snap out of it! It was just a dream," Mike soothed. "Hey, Callie! Hey!"

"Mike," she stammered, wrapping her arms around him. "It was so awful. I can't...oh God. The girl, the little girl. Something happened to her mother. We have to help them, Mike—"

"Help who? Honey, you aren't making any sense. Take a deep breath. It was a nightmare, okay?"

She shook her head. "No. It was more than that. Something's wrong with this place, this house, all of it. I don't want to be here anymore, Mike. Please don't make us stay."

He sighed and pulled her closer as she sobbed into his chest. It didn't seem like he was ever going to take her fears seriously. All she wanted to do was grab her daughter and run from the house, but that wasn't going to happen. Nothing had happened to make Mike understand that the house really was evil. Callie was starting to question her sanity and understood where Benjamin was coming from for the first time. Was it true? Had the house killed him and those poor children? It could have been minutes or hours since the nightmare had gripped her. Time didn't have any meaning.

"Come on," Mike soothed as he pulled her down onto the bed. "Let's get back to sleep, and tomorrow we can talk about our plans."

"I don't want to talk anymore," she whispered. "I just don't want to be here. Not tonight, not tomorrow, not ever. This place…there's something wrong with it."

Mike said nothing as he stroked her head. At first, her worries had seemed like buyer's remorse, but now it was becoming apparent that she would need some help in coping with all the change that had come to their lives. He'd never seen her so distressed. Mike started to hum the same melody she'd used to put Lizzy to sleep almost every night of the young girl's life, and before long, Callie's protests fell silent, replaced by the deep breaths of slumber. There was no way he would be able to get back to sleep, though. It just didn't make any sense why she was fighting so hard to leave Grant Manor. It was the opportunity they'd been searching for their entire lives together.

BY THE NEXT MORNING, Mike knew he would need to start making serious changes to the property if he was going to get Callie to agree to stay. She was still resting peacefully next to him, though she'd tossed and turned a good part of the night. Slipping carefully out of bed, he snuck to Lizzy's room and woke her, helping her to get dressed before the pair headed outside to his waiting pickup. He had a laundry list of things to purchase and get done, all of which would be significantly easier without his loveable little girl riding shotgun, but Callie needed a break.

Plus, the time alone gave him a chance to pick Lizzy's brain and, hopefully, do something to put Callie's mind at ease. The business with their daughter's imaginary friend was what had started everything; maybe he could end it the same way. They bumped along the road as he listened to her talk all about her plans for the manor. He didn't hide his enthusiasm from her. If only they could get her mother to feel the same way they did about the property, everything would be perfect. After they reached the main road, Lizzy ran out of things to talk about and fell silent. He saw the opportunity and dove into the topic.

"So, we haven't heard from your friend much the last few days. Did he move away like the last one?"

Lizzy giggled. "No, Daddy, he's still here. Well, not right here with us but back at the house."

"Oh? He didn't want to come into town? That's a shame, you know. I was thinking about stopping and getting ice cream for breakfast. I bet he'll be disappointed he missed out."

Lizzy rolled her eyes. "*Dad*, he can't eat ice cream, silly!"

Mike gasped in feigned shock. "No ice cream! The horror! Why not?"

"Daddy, he can't eat anything because he's not like us. He's here, but not really. I don't think you'd understand."

He gave her a questioning look. "Oh really, little miss sassy-pants?"

She sighed in frustration, her brow furrowed in concentration as she searched for the words to explain herself. Mike fought the laughter building inside his chest. Despite how serious she obviously took the question, she still looked adorable trying to sort it out. They rode along in silence for a few more minutes until finally, Lizzy let out an exasperated sigh.

"He used to live here. When he was like us, he could get ice cream, but now, he doesn't eat anything. He's not really real."

"That makes sense; he's an imaginary friend—"

"No, he's not!" she yelled.

Mike jumped, shocked by her animated response. "Okay, okay, honey. I'm sorry, I shouldn't have called him that. I know he's your friend. Do we get to know his name?"

"He doesn't remember it," she muttered.

"Oh no? Well, that's too bad."

"It makes him sad. He cries a lot. Sometimes it's so loud that it keeps me awake. He says his sister cries, too, but she remembers her name still. There are lots of things he's forgetting. I think it scares him."

"Awe, well, that's sad. Can we give him a new name? Maybe he'll remember it this time."

"No." She frowned before her eyes lit up. "But I know how we can find out his name! It was on one of the stones in the garden Mommy and I found! Maybe she'll remember it! Oh, Mommy is so smart, I bet that she will...but..."

"But what, sweetheart?"

"He doesn't think we should tell Mommy about him anymore. Last time, she got really upset when she heard me talking to him. That was when we found the stone garden."

Mike's stomach lurched as he sorted through what his daughter was telling him. He didn't remember hearing about any stone garden from Callie. The only places they'd explored since moving in were the woods and the cemetery. Mike pulled the truck over to the side of the road. They were near the edge of town.

"Honey, are you talking about the cemetery?"

She nodded vigorously. "Yes! That's what Mommy called it! What a funny word...."

Mike swallowed. "Is your friend's name Marcus?"

Lizzy gasped. "Daddy! How did you know? Do you see him, too, like Mommy and I do? Yay! Now you can play with us! Do you think you could talk to his sister? She's quiet and not as nice as Marcus, but maybe if she had a mom and dad to talk to, she'd be happy like we are!"

"Sure, honey," he whispered before pulling back out on the road.

His mind was swimming. It was no wonder Callie had been so worked up. Lizzy must have found the children's names somewhere or overheard them speaking. It was the only logical explanation. Then why did she tell him that Callie could see the boy as well? They both knew that Lizzy and her imaginary friends were nothing to be concerned about. For a girl her age, as an only child, it was normal for her to create playmates. Oftentimes, in such situations, kids would act out and blame the deed on whatever "friend" they had at the moment.

It was a good way for parents to teach right from wrong without upsetting the child. Lizzy had already used "Marcus" once to get out of trouble. Mike was sure there would be more incidents in the future. The sooner she grew out of the phase, the better, in his opinion. The entire situation left him with a pit in his stomach, but at least now, he could tell Callie there was nothing to be worried about.

"Daddy?" Lizzy said.

"Yes, sweetheart?"

"I don't think his sister likes us."

"No? Why's that?"

"She keeps playing mean tricks on Mommy, and I

129

don't think Mommy likes them. Well, she scared Mommy in the basement a few days ago, and last night, Marcus said she scared her again in our hiding spot, and that's not very nice."

Mike felt the blood drain from his face. "No," he whispered. "That wasn't very nice of her at all."

21

---

*T*he throbbing pain woke her, though what little sleep she'd managed to get had been riddled with nightmares. Instinctively, she reached for Mike. The sun was already high in the sky, though, and Mike was nowhere to be found. After dragging herself out of bed, Callie found the note he'd left her on the bathroom sink. She smiled at his kindness. Lizzy would enjoy the afternoon with her doting father. Without the pressure of needing to tend to Lizzy, she enjoyed a long shower before starting her day. On a normal day, Callie would rush downstairs and put on a pot of coffee.

With no one around to distract her, though, she instead turned down the hallway in the direction of Mike's study. As the frightening dreams faded in her mind, she was determined to look into what happened to Benjamin and the children. There was too much going on for her to be content with Mike's rationalization. Callie loved her husband, but sometimes he was too stubborn to admit when he was wrong. Instinct and a healthy dose of Catholic superstitions wouldn't allow her to rest easy until she knew the truth.

The door groaned beneath the weight of her hand. Callie loved the space despite still feeling uneasy. It was a sensation she was becoming accustomed to. Back in New York, she wouldn't dream of living in a house that gave her such intensely bad feelings. It was a wonder what people did for love. God willing, Mike would give up on the manor, sell off what they could, and get away from the eccentric town before it was too late.

"Too late for what?" Callie questioned herself. "Jesus, this place is driving me insane. It's no wonder Benjamin went mad."

Finding her way to the plush chair, Callie sat down and tugged open the drawer containing the first round of journals. Her fingers danced across the leather. There were so many of them that she wasn't sure where to start. Plus, if Mike knew she'd been reading them, he would throw a fit and once again accuse her of looking for an excuse to vacate the property. After some consideration, Callie pulled out one at random and flipped it open.

Doc Mathis seems to think I should keep writing, though God only knows why. I never did trust that quack, but Celeste always thought he knew what he was talking about. Damn. Celeste. I still can't believe she's gone. This house feels empty without her. The cops still haven't found his body...I don't think they ever will if I'm being honest with myself. He probably washed down the canal. Maybe he'll surface somewhere along the coast. If he does, I'll burn that bastard for what he did to his mother. She never should have been on the road. Why didn't she listen to me? The bus station is only a few miles north of town. He could have walked or hitched a ride with one of his queer friends.

Callie cringed at the derogatory reference. Mike didn't know much about his grandparents. His father had always insisted they were both dead to him, so what was the point in Mike knowing about them at all? She'd been unable to resist the urge to do a little snooping, though, after they'd been married a few years. While Benjamin's existence had remained a mystery, she was able to find an old newspaper clipping online of the tragic car accident that had claimed his grandmother's life. There had been no mention of Mike's father, though.

My father was right all along. I've got no one to blame but myself. The boy should have gone to boarding school as soon as he was out of diapers, but I let my affection for Celeste cloud my judgment. Look where it got us. She's dead because of my soft heart. If the old man were still alive, he'd tell me it was the curse that claimed her. Women have no place at Grant Manor; they never have. Maybe I should have left this dump when Celeste wanted to. She always did talk about traveling the world when the boy was grown and gone. Well, he's gone now, likely burning in hell where his kind belongs. Frank warned me about going soft on him, but I didn't listen. Lord help me, I never listened. He doesn't know how a woman can change you, though. He doesn't understand how easily their feminine wiles can manipulate a man.

No matter. I've seen him making eyes at the new maid. He'll learn soon enough that women bring nothing but misery to a house...or maybe it's the other way around and the house brings misery to them. What am I saying? I'm starting to sound like Celeste, blaming a useless old heap of brick and stone for her death. No, it was the boy, the bastard. He was no son of mine. I cut him out of the will as soon as I left my dear Celeste's funeral. That junior partner over at the law office thought he could talk me out of it. I reckon he's a fairy, too. They all stick together, protecting their twisted way of life. I hate them. All of them. I will never forgive their kind for taking away my love.

I'll have to remarry, of course. That's the only way for the manor to stay out of the town's hands. If I don't have an heir, it will go to those bastards down at the bank. I'd just as soon burn the place to the ground before I let them get their greedy paws on my family's fortune. Slimy bastards...all of them. Never saw much use for a lawyer. My father would be rolling in his grave if he knew this place didn't have an heir after me. No matter, women are cheap and easy to come by once you flash a few dollars in their direction.

"What a prick," Callie muttered. "A homophobe and misogynist to boot. Poor Mike. Thank God, he never knew you, Benjamin Grant."

A gust of wind moved through the trees, rattling the branches against the window outside. Callie shuddered as she wondered if the dead man could still hear her. In a petty moment, she grinned and snuggled herself deeper into his chair, certain he'd hate the idea of a woman sitting behind his desk. Before she could engross herself in the journal again, someone pounded on the front door. She jumped in surprise before quickly shoving the journal back into its place and darting out of the study. Jogging

134

down the steps, she saw a figure waiting at the entrance. The familiar coloring of the truck outside made her smile. Gavin was fully recovered and had planned to start back to work that morning. Engrossed in the journals, it had completely slipped her mind that he was coming.

"Hey!" she exclaimed, opening the door. "Well, look at you! You'd never be able to tell you were electrocuted a few days ago! How are you feeling?"

He grinned. "Right as rain. Maybe the shock did me a little good, jump-starting my functions and whatnot. You ready to get this place up and running?"

"Not really, but Mike sure does love it. Come on in. He's still in town but should be back any minute. Can I get you a cup of coffee?"

"I sure would appreciate it. That's about the only thing that gets me moving these days."

"Come on, you're too young to be talking like that. You should have the energy of…"

"A dozen volts of electric?" he offered.

She burst into laughter and started for the kitchen as he headed back to his truck for tools. The journals upstairs were calling to her, but maybe Gavin's arrival was for the best. At least it had been him at the door and not Mike walking into the study to find her poring over the words of a man he obviously despised. It was becoming clear that he had good reason. Without ever knowing his grandfather, Mike didn't hold him in very high regard, but Callie was finally starting to understand why his father had kept him guarded and away from Benjamin for all those years.

Her eyes moved to the cubby door as she darted into the pantry. With the coffee grounds and filters in hand, she quickly reminded herself that it had only been a dream. There was nothing to be afraid of in the old house. Still, a wave of unease filled her. The dream came rushing back to her all at once, making her shudder as she closed her eyes and quickly moved back into the kitchen. The house wasn't as bad during the day, though it still had its strange quirks as Mike had called them.

With the coffee brewing, Callie grabbed a pair of mugs and turned to set them onto the counter before freezing. Her smile fell. The mugs in her hand slipped from her grip and shattered on the floor.

She'd forgotten to put away her glass and the bottle of pills from the night before.

It hadn't been a dream at all.

22

"Callie? Whoa! What happened? You okay?"

She jumped, spinning to face Gavin, the trance broken. "Yeah, um, I just...I lost my grip," she muttered. "Jesus, your coffee. I'm sorry. Let me get this mess cleaned up, and I'll have it out in a minute."

"Hey, take your time. You sure you're okay? You look white as a ghost."

Callie cringed but nodded. "I'm fine. Just clumsy, I guess."

"All right, if you're sure you're okay...I'm gonna pop down to old Frank's and see if he's got a pipe saw. I can't seem to find mine anywhere."

"What does it look like? We might have one in the basement."

His eyes widened, his cheeks flushing red with embarrassment. "That's okay, I'll just grab Frank's. I'm still a little leery of being down there alone, honestly."

Callie smiled. "Trust me, I understand completely. I'm not a fan of being anywhere in this place alone."

"Yeah, it's definitely got a mind of its own. Of course, I suppose that's just old superstition. My mom was a big believer in that sort of thing. I don't think I ever really bought into it until…"

"Until the house electrocuted you?"

Gavin gave a slight nod. Callie could sympathize with his trepidations. He disappeared out of the kitchen with some speed as she bent to pick up the larger pieces that had spread across the floor. Was she losing her mind? It felt like it. There was no way Mike would have gotten up in the night and taken the sleeping pills. He'd struggled with addiction as a teen and later with depression. Her heavy prescription was a death sentence for him. Likewise, had he decided to use the pills on some ridiculous whim, he'd have put the bottle back.

No matter how she tried to rationalize the bottle being out, Callie knew it had been placed there the night before by her own hand. Unable to cope with the reality of their situation, she quickly cleaned up the mess and grabbed her coffee and Gavin's before leaving the kitchen again. As she reached the front porch, Gavin was returning with the tool he needed from Frank's. Deep in her subconscious, Callie had half expected him not to return after their conversation. She was relieved to see him. They sat in silence, drinking their coffee and sharing a mutual unease over the manor. The tension only broke when Mike pulled into the driveway.

Elation washed over Callie at the sight of her husband

and daughter. The little girl bounded from the truck, showing off the sack of candy her father had gotten for her. Callie dutifully showed enthusiasm and gratefully accept her daughter's offering of a chocolate bar despite her stomach still being in knots. She quickly noticed that something seemed off with Mike as well, but there was no time for them to talk in private. The men needed to start on the repairs, and she wanted to dive back into Benjamin's journals. Grateful she'd snuck one out of the office in the days prior, Callie settled into the swing while Mike and Gavin started inside and Lizzy ran off into the yard to play.

The journal was dated four months before Benjamin's death. The difference in his handwriting was shocking compared to the journal from earlier in his life. Whether it was old age or the onset of dementia, she couldn't be sure. Where he had taken the time and consideration in his penmanship before, the pages were now spattered with ink spots and poor spelling. Callie racked her mind as she tried to recall the side effects of paranoia. His writing was definitely more akin to the rantings of a mentally unstable man.

Everywhere I turn, people watch me. They all think I've lost my mind, but that's not the case. I bet they're in on it. The whole damn town has it out for me. They still blame me for Maria's death, probably her mother's disappearance as well. I wish they would leave us alone. I've done nothing but give those bastards a cut of my profits over the years. Hell, I could have pulled the lake out from under them at any time. I still might if someone doesn't start giving me answers soon. Wouldn't that be a shock for them if I drained the lake? Their tourism would drop, there would be nothing left of this bullshit little town.

The town my ancestors founded. They should all be bowing to me and begging for forgiveness. Instead, they whisper on the streets. They pretend like I can't hear them, see them, feel them following me. I don't know how they are getting in the house. I've instructed the staff to change all the locks. Whether or not they did so, I don't know. They are probably in on it along with all the others. The doctor wants to put me on medication! Can you believe that? He's calling me crazy...well... he'd never say that to my face, but I know what he's thinking. I know what they're all thinking. I'll kill every last one of them before I let them take my land.

The entry ended with a flourish of curse words. There were several more pages of him ranting before Callie found herself engrossed in the story again. It was obvious to her now that there was something wrong with Benjamin, but his paranoia didn't align with her knowledge of dementia. Yet, he never wrote down what drugs the doctor had tried to put him on or if he decided to take them without penning it in his journal. Lithium was a powerful anti-depressant, though, and one that could cause side effects like paranoia. Still, it was rarely used in the elderly, and by that point in his life, Benjamin could be considered nothing less.

Someone followed me home tonight. They kept their headlights off, but I could see them anyway. I don't know if it was a truck or a car. Hell, it could have been a bike. Whatever it was... it was quiet and stealthy. Even with my windows down and driving slow as a snail, I couldn't make out anything beyond a black shape behind me. They never got close enough for me to see. He was there, though, disappearing as I pulled in. He, she, it —I don't know anymore. All of them. They're in on it together. I know what they want. They want my home and the fortune I've worked for.

They won't get it. Even now, I can hear them moving through the house. They think they are being careful and quiet, but they aren't quiet enough. The staff now looks at me like I'm mad. They walk on eggshells around me. I've fired most of them. Only Frank has stayed behind, bless his heart. I don't know what I'd do without being able to bend his ear. He doesn't think I'm crazy; he's a good man. I've got half a mind to leave him everything in my will. He'll make sure those bastards never get it. No, I can't leave it to Frank. I couldn't even if I wanted, too. The inheritance clause is clear.

No one can own Grant Manor except a Grant. That's why I made sure to adopt the kids. I never wanted to be a father again, and I don't want them to regard me as such. If there were anyone else to leave the land to, I would. I care deeply for the boy and girl, but they aren't my blood. They aren't anyone's blood. Half-bloods is closer. A mix of Maria's Hispanic family and an unknown white guy. Stupid son of a bitch. If she'd told me who it was, I'd have killed him. There is another way...no. I refuse to leave the property to him...

Callie swallowed, jumping a little when Lizzy burst into laughter in the yard. Her eyes darted to her daughter, who had found a friendly barn cat. The calico was rather content sitting on the six-year-old's lap. She could hear the joy in them both as the cat purred and Lizzy told the furry feline all about her new life at Grant Manor.

Knowing Lizzy was content, safe, and just a few yards away from her, she dove back into the old man's story.

I still don't believe that bastard survived the crash. Well, according to my investigator, he was never in the car. Isn't that fitting? His mother loses her life so he can go on to be a fag with his boyfriend. It sounds like he got what was coming to him, though. He's dead in the ground right next to his partner. The irony isn't lost on me. My only regret is that he somehow managed to have a child of his own. There's another Grant running around the world somewhere. I'd sacrifice him in an instant to bring back my Celeste.

23

_____

allie couldn't put down the journal as she continued to read. It skipped ahead several weeks before she caught herself engrossed in it once again. It seemed that Benjamin had regained some control over his mind by the time he had started to write again.

I couldn't take the paranoia anymore. I had to do something about it. After Maria's accident, Frank had suggested that I have cameras installed, but it wasn't something I wanted. The idea of someone being able to watch the children and me on that damn internet wasn't something I approved of. Now, it doesn't seem like I have much choice. I'd love to have Frank help me in installing them, but maybe it's for the best that he's gone to visit his daughter again. Hopefully, by the time he comes back, I'll have some answers about what's going on.

Also, I've found the boy. I don't know what I'm going to do moving forward. I guess all I can do is wait until the cameras are up. Perhaps the village people were right and I'm losing my mind. Either way, we are going to find out. If there is someone following me, the boy and girl won't be safe. I'd rather have that bastard offspring of my blood in the will than risk the kids' lives. They never asked for their mother's death, nor did they think they'd become wards of an old man. All I need to do is get them to eighteen. After that, the bastards here can have me, but I won't go down without a fight, not while Marcus and Vera still live here. I'll kill them all.

His writing was becoming erratic again. His mind didn't seem able to stay focused on a single topic. For three pages, he ranted about the problems of installing cameras as a decrepit old man. A splash of blood on one page accompanied another rant about how he couldn't trust anyone, but the cameras were finally installed, albeit after Benjamin had suffered a fall and needed several stitches. He continued on in such a manner for another four pages, making notes every night after watching the video feed.

"Mommy! Can we go exploring again?" Lizzy asked. "I'm bored!"

"Sure, honey—"

"I want to explore the house this time! Mr. Frank said there were all sorts of fun places to hide inside. Do you think we can find them all?"

Her jaw clenched. The last thing she wanted was Lizzy discovering more places to hide. She'd nearly given them a heart attack on that first night. Plus, with what Callie was learning every day, she didn't want to let her child out of her sight for a single second inside the manor. Yet her curiosity was piqued. When they'd gone through the house upon their arrival, she hadn't seen any cameras.

"I have an idea; why don't we start with the outside of the house? Let's see if we can find any little doors or hidden cubbies. How does that sound?" Callie asked.

Lizzy jumped up in excitement as she vigorously nodded. After giving one last farewell to her new feline friend, they started around the side of the house. While Lizzy bobbed and weaved in and out of the shrubs, searching for hidden gems, Callie kept her eyes trained on the roof and anywhere a camera might have gone unnoticed. They wandered around the outside of the house without Callie finding a single one. Once they reached the porch again, she'd nearly given up the search until a glimmer of white caught her eye.

As Lizzy continued to inspect the brush, Callie inched closer to the object attached to the edge of the roof. There was no camera. Yet, the base for one was still installed. Whoever had removed it had done so hastily. She was determined to solve the mystery of the missing camera, but Lizzy had other plans. The energetic little girl pleaded with her mother to go back down to the lake. Benjamin's words played through Callie's mind, the warning about the lake making her stomach flutter with concern.

"Frank!" Lizzy exclaimed.

Callie jumped and spun around. Once again, the man had moved with such stealth that she hadn't heard his approach from the trail between the two houses. He smiled at the girl. It was obvious he adored children. The death of the two youngsters must have brought him a great deal of pain. Anyone who loved her daughter, Callie would tolerate. Even if she weren't particularly fond of him and his odd personality. If he'd simply open up about what had happened to his former boss, she could have trusted him complicity. As it was, she was leery of him.

"I saw the trucks, thought the fellas could use a hand with whatever project their tackling, but then I saw a few ducks' eggs hatching on my way over and thought of the girl."

Lizzy gasped. "Baby ducks! Mommy, can we go see them? Can we? Pretty please?"

Callie frowned. "I don't know, honey. I wanted to keep exploring the house."

"I could take her if that's okay with you. It's just over yonder. You could see us from here," Frank muttered. He looked wounded.

Guilt surged through Callie. "All right, but don't be gone too long. It's almost time for lunch, okay?" she said.

Frank nodded, his eyes lighting up as Lizzy darted ahead of him. With the few minutes of peace she had, Callie nestled herself back onto the porch swing and flipped open Benjamin's journal again. He'd been telling the truth about installing a camera. Who knew what else he was being honest about? Everyone had written him off as a paranoid old man, but she was starting to wonder if he wasn't the sanest of them all.

I did it. I caught the son of a bitch. I don't know who it is, but I will. The damn camera didn't catch much, but it sure did catch a man walking right up through the front door while we were sleeping. He must have a key. I knew the staff was lying to me about changing the locks. Sure, they changed the ones I told them to, but they must have given him a key or something. I don't know how they did it, but I've got him now. He's after my house...I just know it. The kids aren't safe anymore. I named them in the will. They don't deserve to die for my mistakes. I have to change it; I have to bring back the karma that my bastard son gave me all those years ago. He killed his mother, now it's my turn...

"What in the hell are you talking about?" Callie muttered as she sifted through the jumble of paragraphs.

That's it. The children are safe. I changed the will. Now, if they get me, the kids will be safe. They aren't in the will anymore. There's no reason for the dark man to come after them. He can take whatever deal he's made with the devil in this place and go fuck himself. They won't get the boy and girl. They'll never have them. I watched the cameras again last night. The shadow man had a friend this time. Two women following after him. Following like good little dogs.

I went to the yard this morning, and sure enough, there were three sets of footprints in the snow. They are trying to drive me insane; I know it. That's why they walked around out there without shoes on. Who does that? Who walks around in two feet of snow in their bare feet? I'll tell you who—the bastards who think they can win this. Well, they've got another thing coming. They tried to make me think I was losing my mind. I'm not. I'm not insane. The footprints are there. I took pictures with that damn phone Frank gave me for the holiday.

Took me an hour to figure it out, but boy was he sure shocked when I showed him! He was starting to think I was losing it, too. I wish Celeste had been here to see the shock on his face. Old Frank couldn't believe it! Poor man turned white as a ghost and promised to keep a vigil at night. I don't know what

I'd do without him. He loves those two kids. I know they'll be safe with him even if the people after me win...but they won't. Not now that I know how many of them there are. Those smart bitches stayed off the camera but not their ringleader.

I'm having Frank take the footage to town tomorrow. Maybe the boys in the city will be able to clear it up and give us a face. It's wishful thinking, but hot damn, it feels good to know I'm not insane. Hell, it feels good to know the kids are safe. Now I can't say the same for that "Mike" fella. If anything happens to me, they'll be coming after him next. But the boy and girl are safe; I've kept my promise to their mother, God rest her soul.

Callie gasped. "You terrible old man. You fed us right to the wolves."

24

*H*er mind was swimming. The information was still sinking in when the door to the house opened. Gavin and Mike appeared, laughing and smiling like old friends. She didn't want to tell her husband what she'd discovered. It felt like ages since she'd seen him so happy. The friendship he'd formed with Gavin was understandable. The young man was wonderful and seemed to have a good head on his shoulders. They both stopped long enough to tell her hello before moving back down to Gavin's truck. When he pulled away and Mike returned with a gallon of paint and bag from the hardware store, Callie gave him a quizzical look.

"Is everything okay?" she asked.

"Oh yeah, we've got everything done that we can for now. Gavin's going to grab some lunch and a few more fittings for the downstairs half bath, then we'll get back to it. I figured I'd start painting the basement while I waited."

"Oh, right. I forgot about that. Did you find sealer paint? Is that what it's called?"

He grinned and nodded. "Something like that. The guy said this will stop any leaks and keep the mold at bay from the moisture. Plus, it was on clearance!"

Callie laughed. "God, I love you. Good job—" Her approval was cut short when she saw the splash of color on the top of the can. "Red? Really?"

He shrugged. "Like I said, it was on clearance. Plus, this stuff only comes in red and white. You're supposed to paint over it, which we will. You'll never know it was this color when I'm done, I promise, honey."

"I believe you," Callie muttered.

"Hey now, don't go getting all doom and gloom on me. It's just paint. Wanna come keep me company? Where's Lizzy?"

"Down watching ducklings hatch with Frank."

"Good, he's a good man. Gavin has nothing but great things to say about him. I know he's a little odd, but it seems like he's good with Lizzy."

"I know. I like him, too, but yeah, he's definitely a weird one."

Callie thought about what she'd discovered in Benjamin's journal. She had to talk about it with Mike despite knowing how he was going to react. Helping him in the basement would give her the perfect excuse to bring it up. Tucking the journal beneath the swing cushion before her husband could see it, she jumped up and followed him into the house and down the steps. He had the cellar door to the outside open, letting in a steady stream of light that made the space feel slightly less ominous, though she still wouldn't be caught dead down there alone.

"So, I was thinking…we might be able to open this place up by Thanksgiving. I know we were shooting for a Christmas opening, but honestly, we haven't run into any problems since those electricians left. Gavin sure knows what he's doing."

"Good, that's great news, honey," she mumbled. "Listen, I've been doing a little bit of reading—"

"Uh oh, that's never a good thing," he said playfully.

He popped the lid off the sealer and started to stir it, giving her a wink as he worked. Callie rolled her eyes at him. It felt almost wrong to be breaking his good spirit. She didn't want him to find out about his grandfather on his own, though. If someone were after them, it would be best that they figured it out before he sank all their money into the manor. Even if he got angry at her for snooping into Benjamin's life, at least she'd know she tried.

"Like I said, I've been doing some reading…about your grandfather."

Mike stiffened but said nothing.

"He kept journals and a lot of them. All the way back from before he got married and before your grandmother died—"

"She wasn't my grandmother, and he wasn't my grandfather. I wish you would stop calling them that."

"Fine. Benjamin and Celeste."

"Celeste…" he whispered. "God, that name sounds familiar, but I know I never heard Dad mention her. All right, keep going. So, what did you find? The old man was nuts, right?"

"Well, I'm sure he was a little crazy, but not about someone following him. He actually caught them on camera...."

"What?"

"Yeah, but here's the thing, the camera isn't there anymore. Someone took it down."

"So, all you have is the word of a child killer that someone was following him? Honey, that isn't really solid proof of anything except that he was, in fact, bat-shit crazy. I don't like you reading those things. They are just going to keep you up at night."

Callie cringed. She still hadn't told him about the night before or the bottle from that morning. As a matter of fact, she hadn't given it much thought at all since reading Benjamin's journal. Knowing there was some truth to Benjamin's fears of being followed presented a much more prominent problem.

"Mike, Benjamin Grant didn't leave you the property because he wanted it to stay in the family. He did it to protect Vera and Marcus. He was sure someone was following him, and when he learned he was right about it, he sought you out to protect them."

"So? Who cares? He's gone, and now the house is ours. Why should I care what happened to him?"

"Because he killed two children and he was your blood, whether you like it or not," she snapped.

Mike stood. "Are you okay? Are you sure this is about Benjamin? You haven't been sleeping very well."

"Did you get into my pills last night?" she shot back.

"Of course not. What's this about? You know I don't touch that shit."

"They were out, Mike. As in, I must have taken them out and gotten one last night when I thought it was just a dream, and if that was real, that must mean that whatever that thing was in the cubby was real, too. They are after us, Mike—"

"What's after us?" he snapped. "The ghosts or the boogie man on the camera that doesn't exist. Jesus, Callie. How many times are we going to have to go through this? So, you found the rantings of an old coot and had a bad dream. Is this how things are going to be now? Are we going to fight about this every fucking day?"

"Mike, please don't yell," she whispered, her eyes darting to the cellar steps.

"I'm not yelling yet, but I'm about to start. This has been a good afternoon, but I've about had it. Now your stories are starting to mess with Lizzy, and I've got a problem with that. She's heard us talking, and you took her to a cemetery. Imagine what she's coming up with in that little mind of hers!"

"I didn't mean to take her there; we didn't know what it was, but I don't think her imaginary friend is imaginary at all…."

"Wow. Thanks for putting the pieces together for me. Lizzy mentioned that he wasn't like the others, and now I know where she's getting it from. You need to stop with the ghost stories. She's just a little girl!"

Callie's jaw dropped. "I haven't said anything to her like that. What did she tell you?"

He glared at her. "You know damn well what she told me. Her little 'friend' is named Marcus. Now, where do you think she got that from because it sure as hell wasn't me."

"I...I never said his name to her," Callie stammered. "Mike, there is something wrong with this house. It doesn't want us here."

"It's just a house, and you are just paranoid. I told you I didn't want you reading my grandfather's journals, but you've got no respect for my wishes, now do you?"

Callie was flabbergasted. Mike had a temper, but he'd never spoken to her with so much anger. The house was changing him. She caught his gaze for a split second before he quickly looked away and started to roll paint onto the wall. What she saw sent a chill down her spine. There was something different in his eyes. He looked like he was losing his grip on reality. The frightening sight brought to mind the picture she'd seen of Benjamin Grant on the deceased man's desk.

"I'm sorry. I just thought you'd want to know a little bit about this place and what we are getting ourselves into."

"I want you to burn the journals. Do you hear me? Every last one of them, and if you don't do it, then I will. I'll start locking the study if I can't trust you to stay out of it."

"I'm not a child," she snapped. "I'm your wife. Mike... maybe we should take a weekend away from this place."

"Right," he growled. "You'd like that. Just like a woman to want to spend money but you don't want to work for it. No, leave that to the Grant men. My grandfather was right. Women are evil."

"Mike...you never knew him," she whispered.

25

She stepped away from him. Mike was unrecognizable. Callie moved toward the cellar steps and beam of sunlight coming in from outside. He didn't move to follow her. Instead, he seemed to snap out of the trance, dropping the roller and backing away from it. He shook his head as his eyes sought out his wife. Mike took a step toward Callie, but she took another step away. His gaze filled with fear and instant regret, his jaw becoming slack. She could tell he was shaken by the incident. It wasn't her husband who had snapped at her. No, it was something much more sinister.

"Callie..." he whispered. "I'm so sorry. I don't know what came over me."

"I do," she snapped. "It's this fucking house and that terrible man. He's behind this; I just know it. I don't know if he was murdered or killed himself, but I do know that he was a shit human when he was alive. He was right about one thing, though; this place should be burned to the ground."

"No. I refuse to believe this is all because of some supernatural bullshit. It's the stress, the fatigue from trying to get it off the ground. There are—"

"Just stop it," she growled. "Just stop! Stop making excuses. You know you feel it; you just won't admit it. You want to blame it on everything but what is right in front of you because it means there is a higher power, something out there that you can't explain."

"I think we need to go see someone," he muttered.

"Like a marriage counselor? Yeah, I think we are getting to that point. I'm not going to stay here with my daughter and wait patiently for whatever killed those children to come back and get me or worse, her."

"No, Callie," he said slowly. "I think *you* need to go see someone. I'll go with you if you want, but…this is starting to be a problem, and it's spilling over to Lizzy, too. I don't want to lose you, but I have to think of her."

Her mouth dropped. "Have you lost your mind? You think I'm crazy? That I need to go to a doctor? Mike, this house is evil. I saw something last night in that cubby, that little girl, Vera. She was covered in blood. I'm not crazy."

"Hey," he soothed, "no one is saying you are. I don't like that word. I think the stress of everything is just taking its toll. Maybe it's time you stopped taking the sleeping pills."

"You son of a bitch," Callie hissed. "You are not going to make me out to be the bad guy here. I don't care what you decide to do, but I'm taking Lizzy away from here. We'll go to my friend, Sarah's—"

"For the weekend?" he interjected. "I don't think that's a good idea."

"No, Mike, for as long as it takes for you to see that this place isn't right. Something is off about all of it."

"If you think for one second that I'm going to let you take my family away from me, you've got another thing coming. Tell me, who do you think the local sheriff is going to side with when I call him on you for kidnapping? The man whose name is on the deed or the woman whose seeing dead people?"

"Mike, you don't know what you're saying…."

"No? I don't? Wow, thanks for that great insight, my dear wife. Benjamin told me in my dreams that you were going to be trouble. He said that your kind always was. Catholics, they always think they know everything. I should have left you back in New York, you and Lizzy both. Girls can't be Grants. You're just too weak…too pathetic and emotional."

She could barely breathe. Mike was slipping in and out of whatever psychotic break he was having. Where was the loving and kind man she had married? For a split second, she wondered if she could make a run for it, grab Lizzy and dive into the car. Mike's eyes darted to the steps. He seemed to know what she was thinking. Before either of them could make a move, an eerie wind picked up outside. It rushed the house, grabbing hold of the door and slamming it shut. Callie jumped at the sudden noise.

The only light that illuminated the space now was from the dim bulb.

Mike shook his head, again looking both shocked and terrified of how he was speaking to his wife. She wanted to run to him and wrap him in her arms, but fear kept her feet frozen in place. A sob racked his body as he gasped for air. Callie knew she wasn't alone in her struggles or fears. She only wished that Mike could see that it was driving him mad as well. Grant Manor was digging its claws into the last male heir.

"Callie...I...what do we do? Please don't leave me. Oh, God. Please, Callie," he sobbed.

She ran to him, holding him close as the tears fell from both of them. Her body shook with fear. "It's okay, it's going to be okay," she lied. "We will get through this together."

"Maybe you're right and we need to get away for a couple nights. We'll take the journals and go over them—"

The light above them illuminated with intensity, filling the space with an unnatural amount of light. Callie froze, still wrapped in Mike's arm as they both watched it glowing brighter. Her gut twisted.

"No," she said quickly. "We shouldn't leave. We should stay here."

"What?" he stammered in shock. "I don't under—"

The light started to dim.

"It doesn't want us to leave," Callie whispered.

"I don't care what 'it' wants! I'm going to protect my family!" The light started to glow again, growing more intense as Mike continued. "Screw this place and screw Benjamin Grant!" It flickered. The bulb at the top of the steps jumped to life though neither of them had touched it. "What! You don't like that, you stupid house! Well, fu—"

It burst, shrouding them in darkness as glass fell around them. Callie ducked into Mike's arms as he covered her with his body. She couldn't stop the scream from slipping out. Mike cursed the pitch black as a low hum started to ring in Callie's ears until it became so overpowering, she had to cover them with her hands. Finally, after what felt like an eternity, the noise stopped. They were left alone in the silence.

"We need to leave, now," he whispered.

"Mike, I don't think we're alone anymore."

"Neither do I. It doesn't want us to go…we have to make a break for it. The back steps."

"I don't think that's a good idea," she stammered. "If it doesn't want us to leave, we aren't going to be able to go. This thing, whatever it is, it's strong. I knew it as soon as we set foot in this place. Mike, I think it's the little girl. She's evil. Oh God…what if she's the one who did everything?"

"Then she better stay away from my daughter. Murderous ghost child or not, I won't let anything hurt you or Lizzy. I'm done playing by its rules."

Grabbing his wife's hand, he lunged for the cellar steps, but she was frozen in place. The sudden stop made him turn back to look at his wife. What he saw made his blood run cold as she pointed into the darkness. A small figure had started to take shape, illuminating a faint light from some unknown source. It was too dark to tell what the creature was, though Callie knew. She'd already seen it once before.

"Vera…" she whispered.

"What the hell do you want from us?" Mike yelled.

The figure disappeared at the sound of his voice, only to reappeared seconds later, a few feet closer. Callie could barely breathe. Her chest felt like someone was squeezing her. She didn't realize it was Mike's arms wrapping around her tighter to protect her, clinging to her with as much fear as she held as well. The apparition started to vibrate, its hollow gaze never leaving Callie as Mike continued to yell. She wanted to tell him to stop, she wanted to tell the child to leave them alone, but there wasn't enough air left in her lungs to speak. Mike didn't know what he was doing, but she was slowly starting to lose consciousness. Just as the world around her started to slip into complete darkness, the spirit lunged.

26

"Mike," Callie screamed. "Mike, wake up!"

He groaned, his eyes fluttering open as he sat up on the damp floor. Callie let out a sigh of relief to see him coming back around. The last few minutes had been a blur after she had passed out. She woke to find Mike lying next to her, a small cut on his hand but otherwise uninjured. The light at the top of the steps gave off its usual dull glow, though the one above them was completely busted. She still wasn't sure how the light at the top of the steps had turned on, but it was the least of her concerns. All she wanted to do was get out of there as fast as possible.

"What the hell happened?"

"I don't know. You must have scared her off. We need to go."

"What? Who? What's going on?"

Callie's heart dropped. "You don't remember seeing her?"

"Who?"

"Vera, Mike. She was right over there."

"You mean the kid Benjamin killed? Honey, I think you must have hit your head. Listen, this house is weird and all but—"

The cellar door opened, the bright light nearly blinding them both after being in the darkness so long. Callie shielded her eyes, still struggling to wrap her head around what Mike had said. How could he not remember? Frank appeared at the base of the steps, yelling down and asking if they were okay. He'd seen the wind gust knock the door closed.

"Took me a good twenty minutes just to get it open again."

"Twenty minutes? We just got down here," Mike replied. "Callie, what were you saying about Vera?"

Callie shook her head. "Nothing. We should go check on Lizzy."

"Whoa, doing a little painting, are you?" Asked Frank. "I gotta say, I've heard of some funny techniques, but I don't think writing on the wall is one of them."

"What are you..." Mike started. "Callie, did you write that?"

She spun around to look where Mike was pointing and shook her head.

"No, you were squeezing me so hard that I passed out. It looks like a child wrote it."

"Well, now that just plum don't make any sense. Little Liz was outside with me the whole time. Now, Mrs. Grant, if this is your idea of a joke—"

"I didn't write it," Callie snapped at Frank.

"Heh…heal…help! It says help, Mommy!" Lizzy proudly said as she sounded out the two words.

"Help. Us." Lizzy pursed her lips in confusion. "Mommy, what does that mean? Does someone need help? If so, we should help them. You always say the best thing we can do for our own soul is helping others, right?"

"Honey, why don't you go check on the ducks again?" Callie said.

"But, Mom—"

"You heard your mother, go on," Frank sternly said.

The little girl rolled her eyes and stormed back out of the cellar. Callie approached the wet paint. It was definitely written by a child, but why was she asking for help when just a few seconds ago she was trying to kill them both. With Mike still not remembering what had just happened, she ran through everything in her mind over and over again. There had to be something she was missing. Of course, the spirits were upset. They'd been murdered by a man they trusted. Benjamin was their guardian, a man they loved. The whole situation made Callie sick to her stomach. She could never hurt another living soul.

"Oh my God," she whispered before spinning to Frank. "Thank you so much for your help, Frank, but would you mind giving us a few seconds to talk? Gavin will be back any minute, and I know he's not fond of the basement."

"Sure," he muttered.

Callie waited for him to leave before turning to her husband. "Mike, I think—"

"I remember what happened now. I remember it all. My God," he interrupted. "I saw her, too. What the hell is going on? We need to get the hell away from this place. I don't want Lizzy...Jesus, Lizzy. That means her little friend really is a gh...well, not imaginary. I was so mean to you, sweetheart. Can you ever forgive me? What if that thing tries to hurt Lizzy or one of us again? She just knocked me out cold!"

"I don't think she was trying to hurt either of us. Mike, you were squeezing me so hard that I was passing out. I think she lunged at you to try to save me. It's you, Mike. Every time you get angry, Vera can sense it and it scares her. That's why the light blew out when you were getting so upset earlier."

"So, she has a problem with men, great," he said.

"No, she doesn't have a problem with men. She had a problem with men hurting women. I think her father or whomever her mother was with was abusive. She's asking us for help."

"Help with what? We already know who killed them—"

"But what if we don't? What if your grandfather wasn't crazy after all and there is something to his story of being followed? He said he caught the people on camera."

"This is really upsetting you, isn't it?"

"Isn't it upsetting you? If it's not, then it damned well should be. We're living in a freaking haunted house, for Christ's sake!"

"No, I didn't mean like that. Of course, it's messing with me, too. This is so much to take in all at once. I just meant the kids…them dying…that's different. You don't think it was Benjamin anymore?"

She shook her head. "No, I don't think so, and I think that's what they've been trying to tell us…well, me at least and Lizzy. The boy talks to her. Benjamin was right about being followed, but he wasn't the killer. Whoever did this wanted the property and must not have known that the will changed to your name. They don't want us out; they want us to help them."

"So, they really are little Casper's," he said with a grin.

Callie groaned and rolled her eyes. "Come on, let's get out of this basement and get some fresh air."

"Hey, have you noticed something? It doesn't feel all creepy and weird like it did before," Mike said.

Callie paused for a moment, taking in her surroundings before nodding in agreement. It seemed like now that they knew what Vera wanted, the entire atmosphere of the manor had changed. Granted, Benjamin had still been a terrible person full of faults, but it was starting to look like he wasn't the killer everyone had painted him to be. They emerged just as Gavin pulled up.

"Let's table this until tonight," Mike whispered as Gavin and Frank approached. "I don't know why, but this feels like something we need to talk about and research on our own. Gavin is a nice kid, but now I'm questioning everything."

"Sounds good," Callie replied as she took his hand. "I'm just happy we are on the same page again."

Mike cringed and pulled her to a halt before the others could approach. "Callie. I'm so sorry I didn't believe you before. I've never seen anything like that. Her nightgown was covered in blood. God, the blood…and did you see that gash in her neck? She must have put up a fight, too. One of her nails was missing. I tell you what. When we figure out what really happened, I'm going to have a séance and throw those kids a party. Poor little—"

She stood on the tips of her toes and planted a kiss on his lips to silence him, a playful smile appearing. It felt like a weight had been lifted off her shoulders just knowing they were back to being a team.

"Don't worry about it, okay? I wouldn't have believed me either until I saw it with my own eyes."

"Yeah, and now that I have…" Mike shuddered. "Let's figure this riddle out and get away from this place."

Callie's eyes widened in shock. "You mean it? We can help them?"

He grinned. "I might be a Grant, but I'm not Benjamin. Of course, we'll help."

27

"I still don't understand what was wrong with me," Mike admitted. "It felt like there was this darkness inside of me. It was like...I knew what I was saying, but in the moment, there was just rage. It was awful. I was so angry."

Callie shuddered as she recalled what had happened. The way he had verbally abused her was haunting even now, knowing that it wasn't her beloved husband speaking. She was certain of who it had been. The way he'd talked matched up with the writings of Benjamin Grant.

"I think if the two children are trapped here, Benjamin must be as well."

"But wouldn't he want to help us, too? His spirit—or whatever you want to call it—wasn't exactly grateful to have us here, trying to connect."

"I think that might just be who he is, or was, Mike," she replied. "You should read some of his journals. He wasn't exactly a loving and caring man. Having a woman speak to a 'Grant man' the way I do must have ruffled his feathers."

"You can say that again," Mike muttered. "If it weren't for those kids, I'd say screw it and just have an exorcism done. He definitely wasn't a nice guy."

Callie smiled. "Well, I think the first thing we need to do is find out more about this property and your grandfather's murder. How could anyone call it suicide without being completely sure? Talk to the local sheriff; I'm sure they'll help us out."

"I'd like to know more about Benjamin and what went on around here. If he's going to be making regular appearances, I want to be prepared. Do you think you could dive into his journals a little more? Honestly, I don't want to get that close to the office."

She reached out and squeezed his hand. "Of course I can, sweetheart. What are we going to do about Lizzy? I don't want to leave her alone, not with everything we know."

Mike shrugged. "She loves Frank. Why not ask him to keep an eye on her. He seems to adore her, and they never get too far away."

"I don't know...."

Lizzy waved to her mother from the edge of the water. Frank was positively beaming as the little girl caught tadpoles. He'd been visiting family when they had first arrived. It was evident he loved children. Despite him being slightly off-putting toward her, Callie couldn't complain about the aged groundskeeper. After spending some time with Benjamin's journals, she could understand Frank's personality a bit better. He was raised in the same era. It had to be hard adjusting to a family like theirs. Everything they did, they did as a team.

"Come on, Callie. He's like a hundred years old...." Mike said with a grin.

She giggled. "All right, but would you mind asking him? I think he likes you a little bit better. If they could stay where I could see them—"

"I've got it, honey," Mike said quickly.

He gave his wife a peck on the cheek and jogged across the side yard to the lake. When the pair of men looked back at her, Callie waved before slipping inside. Now that she had Mike's blessing to go through the journals, she was excited to get started. A cold chill moved through her as she sat down in the chair. It felt like someone was watching her. Her gaze quickly moved outside the windows, but Frank and Lizzy were engrossed in the lake's wildlife.

The chill was a stark reminder that she wasn't alone in the house. Despite the only breathing creatures being rodents and the occasional trapped insect, she felt watched. Part of her wanted to reach out to the void and ask who was with her, yet the rest of her was terrified of the answer that might come. Instead, she turned her attention to the journals, though the sensation of being watched never left her side. With a sense of purpose, Callie sought out any mention of the children.

It's hard to believe it's been three years since Celeste passed. Not a day goes by that I don't think about her. Some of the men at the country club ask me about getting remarried, but I won't hear of it. What's the point in giving a woman the Grant name when she can't do anything for me? No, Celeste and I made the decision long ago that there would be no more children. She did her due diligence in giving me the boy. It wasn't her fault the way he turned out...at least not entirely. I'm sure it was just another cruel joke on me by the big man upstairs.

Too bad for him I won't go down without a fight. No matter. I was happy to have the boys snipped when Celeste asked me. I'm too damn old to go having things reversed now. No, the Grant Manor will die with me. I'll be damned if I can't get away from the hounding of getting married lately. That damn woman I took up to clean the manor is after me, too. Damn. Mae is a fine woman. Shame her bloodline isn't better. I'd have married her in a heartbeat. She's fertile. I'm sure we could come to some sort of arrangement. No, another cruel twist of fate on my part. Leave it to me to have tender feelings for the damn help. She probably snuck across the border like the rest of them.

Callie ground her teeth together. It wasn't the first time she'd wished the old man was alive so she could give him a piece of her mind. She jumped ahead a few pages. If she wanted the rantings of an old racist, there were politicians she could watch on television. How any woman could find him charming or attractive was beyond her. When she saw the woman's name again, she started reading; hoping the rant was over.

I've found myself growing more fond of Mae with each passing day. She's unlike any woman I've ever met. Even my dear Celeste wouldn't understand the fascination I feel for the spicy young woman. Mae lights a passion inside of me I dare say I've never felt before. It doesn't change anything; marriage is still out of the question, but she doesn't seem to worry about it any longer. Even Frank has taken a shine to her. I'll have to tell him about Mae and me eventually. My oldest friend deserves to know. I think he might be a bit soft for Mae. I'd hate for him to be the center of an embarrassing moment should he pursue his affections. Yes. Maybe it's time for me to tell him.

Callie checked the dates on the entry. Several weeks passed before he wrote in his journal again. Outside, Lizzy could be heard laughing. It warmed Callie's heart, though she felt a little guilty for reading into Benjamin's history, knowing Frank played such an intricate part in the old man's stories.

How foolish I had been to think Mae would understand. Last night was the worst fight we've had yet. Her hot temper sets me off every time. There is nothing wrong with our relationship, or at least that's what I thought, but she's determined to break me. I'm starting to wonder if she only loves me for the Grant fortune. No matter, if she wants to have her tantrum and leave, then so be it. She was nothing more than a maid anyway. I certainly hope she doesn't plan on asking for a reference letter, though she did have a very particularly good set of skills—"

Callie slammed the journal shut, not wanting to know what Benjamin wrote next. Whoever Mae had been, she seemed to just be a passing fancy. Cracking open the book again, she glanced carefully down a few paragraphs until the content was no longer risqué.

How that woman toys with me. She doesn't think I know what happened that night, but I do. I've made it clear that things are over between us, but she can stay on and care for the house until the time comes for her to deal with the problem at hand. Mae honestly thought I would believe that she was faith-ful. The poor fool's face when I explained I couldn't have chil-dren was priceless. I should have trusted my gut. Women can't be trusted. But I'm no monster. I won't turn her out as she deserves. She swears she doesn't know who the real father is.

Her excuse? They were both drunk on watermelon whiskey. Firewater. Poison. She claims he had on a mask. I wouldn't care if it was the Pope's baby she was carrying, it's not mine, and I want nothing to do with it.

"Dear God, Benjamin Grant, you really were a prick of a man," Callie muttered.

A gust of wind shot through the room, forcing open the shutters as several books swept across the room. Callie jumped but stayed in the seat. She refused to be bullied by a dead man. Nothing was going to stop her from getting the truth.

28

*T*ime seemed to pass without much happening for the next twenty years. Benjamin's entries became less violent and hateful as Mae had her child, a little girl she named Maria. Benjamin even allowed the pair to stay on at the manor and continue working. Despite himself, it was evident that he cared greatly for the woman and girl, yet he always kept them at arm's length. Mae's tryst with the stranger in the bar seemed to be enough to end all of Benjamin's interest in her. It wasn't until Maria became pregnant that the entries became anything more than the daily stats for the property and stock market.

By then, Callie was down to the final three journals, including the one still stashed beneath her bed. It was the one she'd taken out on their first night yet hadn't had the chance to start reading it. The journal had been his last. It only seemed fitting that she should save it for the end. The leather-bound book seemed to carry with it the weight of the manor itself. Even thinking about retrieving it sent a chill through Callie's body. Instead, she dove back into the last few that she had in the office. Perhaps the final one would be a good one to wait and read together with Mike.

Mae has been missing since yesterday morning. I asked Maria if her people went off on their own to pass away, but she gave me a look that indicated I'd stepped out of line once again. I don't know how Maria puts up with me. I couldn't imagine the last twenty years without Mae and her looking over me. Of course, I'd deny that to the devil himself if he asked me. Reckon I should be as worried as Maria seems to be, but I'm just not. Women have a way of wandering off when it comes to Grant Manor. If the house doesn't get them, then the land will. At least Celeste never saw it coming. She didn't think the house would go after her so far away.

Maria went and brought in the law. They're not much help. She called them a few choice words in Spanish and gave me a bit of a laugh. The girl always could bring a smile to my face. Those two brats of hers are enough to drive an old man insane, though. They seem to get into everything. Of course, Frank's taken a liking to them. It's no wonder considering...no. That's a secret I'll take to my grave, and by the looks of things, Grant Manor is starting to pick us off one by one. I don't know if I'm next, but I'm sure I'm not far down on the list.

The more Callie read, the more she wondered if he really had gone insane. He seemed adamant that the house possessed some sort of evil or curse beyond his own spirit and negativity.

How long will it be before none of us are left standing?

Maybe that's what the place wants, a way for it to finally all end. Shame that bastard died with his mother, my beloved Celeste. At least if he were still around, I could have run off with Mae years ago and been done with the wretched Grant name. Now Mae's gone, and this place has a hold of my old bones.

I'm at my wit's end with the local law. They've never given two shits about the Grant family. I think they're still bitter over us refusing to let them use the land for training exercises. I tell you what, though, that's the last thing I want is a bunch of rookies with guns running around my woods. With the kids just now getting curious about the water, it would be a damned shame to lose one of them. That's Maria's biggest fear—the water. I've tried a dozen times over the years to get her to take swimming lessons, but she won't hear of it.

She's stubborn that one, just like her momma. I wish they would take Frank and me seriously about Mae. It's not like her to leave without telling us. I've asked Maria about people from their home country, but she insists her mother never spoke of it. Though Frank has hinted a time or two that Mae still had connections down south. Did they track her down? She would do anything to protect Maria. Anything at all. I wonder if someone knew that?

Callie took a deep breath. She knew they had never found Mae. As soon as Callie had learned about Maria's mother, she'd pulled up old newspapers on the woman just as she'd done before with Celeste's death. The case was closed not long after Mae went missing, with no outcome or effort from the local police. They'd simply listed her as a missing person, most likely running from the immigration office. Years later, a death certificate was quietly listed in the obituaries, assumingly having gone unnoticed by all but Benjamin, Maria, and Frank until Callie had found it.

Her heart ached for all those involved. She knew the tragedy that would continue to follow Maria and Benjamin. It made her sick to her stomach, yet she knew she had to press on. All she could do for them now was help them to find their final peace and get justice for their true killer, even if it ended up being the very manor they all loved. No. There had to be a plausible explanation. Houses didn't kill people any more than weapons did. If there were evil in the house, it was brought by someone intentionally.

It's been a year since Mae went missing. Frank changed after that. I don't think he ever stopped loving her despite him never sharing his feelings with her. She would have told me. I think we are all assuming the worst at this point. Maria won't let the little ones out of her sight. She's still confident her mother is alive. I won't be the one to break her heart, but it's looking bleak at this point. Frank, God bless him, has taken her and the twins under his wing. He's a grandfather at heart, that man.

A letter came for Maria today. I opened it without thinking when I saw where it was from. Good thing I did, too. It was from someone down south claiming to know Mae and what happened to her. Suffice to say that we will never find her body, but I fear our worst nightmare has come true—Mae is dead. It seemed she had a sordid life before coming to us. You'd never know from her sweet temperament in her later years. A damn shame. I'll have to think of something to tell

Maria, although I'm quite certain she knows she's gone forever.

She had to take a break. The pain she still heard in Benjamin's voice shook her body. The room felt darker somehow, knowing what the man had endured over the years. It did seem like he had the worst luck when it came to women. First his wife, then later, Mae. The children... thank God he was dead before their demise came about. She was sure he didn't kill them, not after everything he'd already been through and the people he lost.

Stretching out her limbs, Callie meandered over to the window and looked out over the lake. True to his word, Frank had kept their adventure to where Callie could see them from the house. He, too, had suffered so much over the years. Her heart lurched for Frank. Once they figured out what had happened to Benjamin and the twins, hopefully, it would bring Frank some peace and he could retire. If anyone deserved to forget all their worries, it was him.

Frank stood over Lizzy, who had crouched down in her now dirty dress to pet something on the ground. A gentle breeze moved through the trees lining either side of the lake. Movement near the edge caught Callie's watchful gaze. Her eyes struggled to focus on the figures at the edge of the trees. The antique glass created a film over them. From what she could see, there were two people. Unhooking the latch, she slowly pushed open the window. Her stomach dropped when the blurred figures remained unchanged. The shapes walked with feminine movements.

Callie wanted to scream out and warn the two by the water, but the air in the room suddenly felt suffocating. She grabbed her throat, fighting for a breath as the figures moved closer to her little girl and caretaker. Callie bolted away from the window and through the door. The grip on her throat released the second she crossed the threshold. She raced to Frank and Lizzy, her eyes darting around frantically for the shadow figures, but they were nowhere to be seen. She wrapped her arms around Lizzy, racing away from the dark water to the house she feared almost as much.

"There was more than one of them. Something isn't right here, Mike," Callie hissed into the phone. "I thought I knew what we were dealing with, but now I'm not so sure. I just, I don't know, can you please just come home? Maybe this is a bad idea."

"No," Mike growled. "I've been waiting to meet with this asshole for over an hour. Now it's personal. You'd think I was a leper the way these people reacted to hearing my last name. Jesus, Callie, what is wrong with this town?"

"So much," she muttered. "I don't know what to do, Mike. I don't want Lizzy out of my sight. I'm sure of what I saw. I just wish it made sense."

"Well, we thought the twins were after her to start with, too. Maybe these news ones are the same and they don't have any malice?"

"I don't know. I wish I could believe that, but you didn't see the way they were moving. I felt the darkness

180

dripping off them even from where I was standing. It was so weird. I just...I don't know anymore. I'm just going to keep her with me until you get home. If we had another car, I'd be leaving and coming into the city to be with you right now."

"Now, sweetheart, we knew this was going to get dicey, but what can we do now? You don't want to leave those...you don't want to leave things the way they are. You'd never be able to live with yourself."

"Yeah, well, living with guilt is still better than not living at all," Callie muttered.

"I'm sure those poor creatures would feel the same way. I'm not saying we have to stay if you feel uncomfortable; I just want to make sure this is what you really want."

She sighed, her head already spinning with the options, though she knew they couldn't leave. Something was holding her there, all of them. They wanted and needed Mike and Callie's help. The figures outside still terrified her, but it wasn't as if she were helpless. Being raised in a devout family had its advantages. She'd brought with her everything they needed to bless the house, a family tradition she always carried out.

With everything that had been happening, though, it had slipped her mind. While she was sure it wouldn't get rid of the activity, at the very least, they'd feel a little safer. Callie briefly thought about letting Lizzy sleep in her and Mike's room, but she knew the girl would never go for it. She'd made friends with the ghost boy and was enjoying the time they got to spend talking now that her parents had stopped questioning her about him all the time.

"I want to stay. I know we need to finish this. I just wish my stomach would stop rolling all the time. Does it think I don't know what the dangers are? It's just getting old, I guess. I was starting to wonder if you'd been arrested, too. I didn't realize how much time had passed."

"At least if I'd gotten arrested, one of these assholes would probably be talking to me. I swear they were all sunshine and rainbows until I told them who I was; now it's nothing but silence."

"So, what are you doing?"

"Waiting on the damn person in charge. They act like I haven't been here all morning. They literally went to the guy's door, told him I was here, and nothing changed. It's not like he snuck out the back for some emergency. The son of a bitch is just making me sit here and wait. I've got half a mind—"

"To keep sitting there and waiting?" Callie offered. "Remember why we are doing this. If they're being jerks about things already, then that makes them look pretty suspicious in my eyes. You've always been good at sleuth work for your books. Make them squirm."

Mike laughed. "I never thought I'd have to use it like this, though."

"Well, good luck. I think Lizzy and I are going to take a walk down the road and meet our new neighbors. I know there is a house at the corner where it turns into the state route."

"Just be careful. Not many people travel down that road, but the few who do really fly."

"You mean you and Gavin?" Callie asked.

He chuckled. "Yeah, and I bet you will too once we get you your own car. Enjoy your walk, and make sure you take some water. Who knows, you two might have to hitch a ride here in a while and come bail me out if I don't start getting some answers soon."

"Maybe you should put Gavin in your speed dial then. I don't think anyone out here is going to give us a lift," Callie reminded him. "They'd barely slow down once they realized who we were. You should ask the sheriff what in the hell is wrong with these people while you're at it."

"Right? Assuming I don't die of old age first," Mike replied.

"Careful, around here, it might be ruled a suicide."

Mike laughed on the other end. Callie's heart soared. It felt good to be in sync with her husband again. Keeping secrets from him was never Callie's first choice. Their relationship had always been built on a foundation of openness and honesty. Now that Mike understood and felt first-hand, he could relate to her in a way that garnered solidarity. Ending the call, Callie gathered up Lizzy, and they set off down the driveway.

Frank watched them from his porch. She was sure his curious nature would get the better of him and he'd come to the main house to see which direction they headed. The nosey nature would have bothered her a few weeks prior, but now she found comfort in knowing he cared so much. He was an eccentric old man but had yet to prove anything other than harmless. Lizzy darted ahead of Callie, but she didn't worry. It was rarely a road people traveled on. With the flat terrain, they could see a car coming for miles.

As they moved away from the Grant property line, Callie felt a noticeable tension leave the air. It was no wonder people steered clear of the place. At that moment, she realized she hadn't left the property since coming there. How many other women fell into the manor's trap, only to never leave again? She pushed the thought from her mind. They were working on it. Hopefully, their hard work and Mike's time in town would prove useful toward that goal.

A short time later, after Lizzy had collected a bouquet of wildflowers for their new neighbor, the duo wandered up a gravel driveway. From the road, the house seemed to be in good shape. It wasn't until they got closer that Callie saw it needed some care. Lizzy excitedly knocked on the door. Inside, the sound of shuffling feet could be heard moving about before a curtain off one window fluttered.

Callie waved at the elderly woman but was met with a scowl. Her heart sank. Just once, it would be nice to be met with a pleasant response. She was starting to question if that would ever happen in the tight-knit community. After some time, the door opened a crack, and the woman glared out at them again. She looked Callie up and down before clenching her jaw. It was obvious she hadn't been expecting company.

"What do you want?" she barked.

Callie forced herself to smile. "HI there! My name is Callie, and this is Lizzy Grant—"

"I know who you are. I asked what you wanted."

"Right," she muttered. "Well, we're new to the area and just wanted to get to know our neighbors. It's an interesting old property. Do you know much about the previous owner?"

"You mean your monster of a grandfather? Of course, I do, and you should be ashamed of yourself for not burning that place to the ground with his memory the second you laid eyes on it."

Callie grinned. "Actually, Benjamin Grant was my husband's grandfather, and neither of us knew him. I can tell you from reading his journals, though, I agree with you. He was a crap human."

The woman gave Callie a second look. Callie knew she was still on the fence.

"Listen, I'm just trying to figure out what the heck is going on with that place. I don't want to be there any more than you want us; I can promise you that. Help me figure this out, and I'll invite you to the burning ceremony, okay? I just want to know what you've seen and heard over the years."

"I've been here a long time, my entire life. That story might take a while."

"We've got all the time in the world," Callie assured her.

"Fine," the woman grumbled. "Let me put on some tea, and I'll be right out. This isn't a story for kids, though. She might as well go play with the kittens we had born a few weeks back."

Lizzy's eyes lit up in excitement as the woman pointed to the open garage door. Callie could already see a few curious little eyes peeking out at the commotion. As soon as Lizzy approached them, four more appeared and became quick friends with the little girl. Callie settled onto the porch and shot Mike a quick text. At last, they were getting somewhere.

hen the woman returned with a tray, Callie helped her set up the tea before settling back in. The porch furniture, much like the rest of the property, needed a good bit of work. Callie couldn't help but think of Gavin. It was the type of thing he loved to do and would surely help the woman out for a fraction of what someone else would charge. Making a mental note to mention it to Gavin, Callie waited for the woman to share her story.

"So you said you knew Benjamin and his wife?" Callie asked.

She nodded. "I was engaged to Benjamin Grant, you know. A long time ago. Long before he killed Celeste and her son. I'm so old, I can't tell you the boy's name. After they passed, it was too hard to keep the memories alive. I knew Benjamin, though, when we were all young. My parents and his were always close.

"Those four just adored the idea of us getting married.

I suspect my parents a little more than his. I was no Southern belle after all. No, my father came into some inheritance money and got it in his head that he was going to make it big in the oil business. Thank God my momma had the sense to tuck some away in a trust for me.

"Otherwise, I'd have lost the house years ago. I suppose I still dodged a bullet when I caught Celeste and Benjamin behind the barn that night. He pleaded with me to still get married, as did my parents, but I wouldn't hear of it. Celeste loved him, and he loved her. It wasn't my place to interfere. I'm sorry, I'm getting off track here. You don't want to hear about my family."

"No, it's fine, really. My husband is a writer. I love listening to people talk. That's how we fell in love."

"Hmm, you'd be smart to get that love out of there before something bad happens. That's the truth of the matter. I've never met a woman who came back out the same."

"What do you think happens to them?"

She shrugged. "Any opinions of mine are just the rantings of an old coot. No one ever listens to me about that place or that family. Celeste didn't and look how she ended up. Mae didn't stand a chance, a shame...she was such a pretty little thing. I'm sorry, you'll be wondering who that is?"

"No," Callie said. "Actually, I've been reading Benjamin's old journals. Do you know what happened to Maria?"

She swallowed. "You'd be better off asking Frank about that if he's still lurking about."

"Frank? Why?"

"He's the one who found the poor girl's body. I can't imagine something like that happening to a good man like him not once but twice? After finding the twins and old Ben, we were sure he'd never come back…guess the place would run without him, though…."

"So Frank found her? She drowned, right?"

"Sure did, but I don't know if I believe that, either. I think that land was cursed the second the Grants bought it. You can take it back as far as you want, but the real problems started when Benjamin's father took over the place. You've read his journals. Well, a man doesn't become someone like that without learning it from someone and his daddy was a right mean soul."

"I haven't heard much about his father or his mother, for that matter. He never mentions them in his journals."

"I can't say that I blame him. His father had a nasty temper but drenched the town in money. He could get away with murder, and I'm damn sure he did a time or two. Benjamin wanted to be just like his old man. His mother, God rest her soul, was a docile creature. Benjamin said she lost her mind in the later years and jumped from a window. His father couldn't take it after that and just up and left, disappeared. Left the estate to Benjamin then."

"And Celeste," Callie correct. "It was marital property. This state considers it both partners equally."

She chuckled. "Sure, if it hasn't been grandfathered in.

No woman has owned Grant land in as long as the history books can remember, child. You look over that deed with a keen eye, and you'll see it real quick."

Callie swallowed and fell silent. She was kicking herself for not reading the stack of paperwork Mike had given her to sign before taking out the loan. Was it true? Did she own nothing now? Her cheeks felt warm. Had Mike known, he would have told her. At least he would have back in New York, but who knew how long Benjamin Grant's spirit had been toying with her husband's mind. Without anything in her name, she was trapped. Even if Mike and she continued on joyfully for the next twenty years, that knowledge would linger in her mind. She quickly checked her phone, but Mike still hadn't replied.

"Was there anything, in particular, you wanted to know about?" the woman asked.

Callie shook her head. "No, you've been incredibly helpful. I think we should probably get going. My husband should be home soon."

"Well, if you ever feel like hearing more, you know where to find me."

"Oh, I'd love to come back," Callie admitted. "How's tomorrow for you? We can make it another trip. I think you've found a fan of those kittens in Lizzy."

The woman smiled. "She's welcome to play with them whenever she wants. My name is Deloris, by the way. Keep an eye on your little one out at that place."

Callie swallowed as she recalled the figures from before. She nodded in unspoken understanding. Lizzy was her life, her entire world, without question. They waved a final farewell to their new friends, both human and feline, before Lizzy skipped ahead of Callie down the driveway. The road was just as deserted as it had been on the way down.

She watched as Lizzy darted between the road and neighboring fields. The honeysuckle was in full bloom. It gave Lizzy a sweet distraction from her mother's attention, leaving Callie time to think about the home they were returning to. It would be impossible now to let the little girl out of her sight. Even if they solved the mystery of Benjamin and the twin's deaths, there was a darkness that continued to linger.

That fact was proven by the figures Callie had seen earlier. If only she'd been able to make out who they were. At least then, she'd be able to scan old court records for anyone who might have died on the property. As it was, the only person she had left to talk to was Frank. If they were going to solve the mystery, she would need his help in doing so. Despite his off-putting temperament, Frank had proven that he loved anyone with the last name Grant.

Before long, they were turning back down the driveway. To Callie's happy surprise, Frank was at the end of the driveway trimming the hedges. She didn't believe for a second that it was pure luck. No, Frank was the kind of man to be watchful of Lizzy and Callie as well. Letting Lizzy run ahead a bit, Callie settled her resolve to ask him about the manor before she and Mike had taken it over.

Still, she wasn't expecting him to be much help, given their last conversation about it.

"We met our neighbor today. She seems like an interesting lady. She had nothing but nice things to say about you," Callie offered.

Frank grunted. "That crazy old loon wouldn't know me from a lineup. She lost her mind a long time ago with all that ghost nonsense. I think she needs to be in a home, but no one around here will listen to me."

"She seemed sweet," Callie muttered.

"I'm starting to think you just like seeing the best in people and places. I know you've been digging around about the murders that took place here. I don't think you're going to find what you're looking for. I cared for old Ben and those kids, but it's time that you let sleeping dogs lie."

Callie ground her teeth. Frank was starting to sound like Benjamin in his journals. She crossed her arms over her chest and stopped walking long enough for frank to pause and look back at her.

"Tell me about Mae, or I'll go ask someone else," she snapped.

Frank went pale, his eyes traveling past Callie to the tree line. "Mae," he whispered. "She'll haunt me until the day I die."

*M*ike tapped his fingers on the waiting room chair, well aware of the ire it was causing the office at the desk behind him. Not once had he seen movement from the chief's office, though there was no other entrance or exit from the building that Mike couldn't see from where he sat. He'd already decided to give it another five minutes. After that, he'd get the chief's attention in a different way. Callie had thought he was joking, but no, if an arrest was what it would take to get answers, so be it.

The officer behind the desk shot him another well-deserved glare. Mike grinned at the man. The cop's cheeks flushed bright red before he shot up from his desk and stormed to the chief's door for a second time. Mike couldn't hear what he was whispering, but it didn't seem to be well received. He sulked back to his seat, shooting one final look at Mike before returning to his work. Mike counted down the seconds, his anger growing with each pass of the second hand on the dilapidated wall-clock. Another sixty seconds and he was going to lose his cool.

The forbidden door opened, and to Mike's shock, a woman near her fifties emerged. She wore the insignia of a police chief, though her robust frame made him doubt her ability to pass a physical. She brandished the same cheerful scowl as her subordinate at the front desk. Had it not been for the hateful look on her face, she'd be an attractive woman. It was apparent from her stature that she enjoyed the power that came with running the small town and police headquarters.

He cleared his throat when it became evident that she wasn't going to acknowledge him. Her entire body stiffened, struck with indignation. For such a reaction, one would think Mike had insulted her out loud. One hand flew to her hip, her brow arching as she looked Mike up and down. Mike forced himself to smile. He stood and approached the desk with his most charming smile.

"Morning, ma'am," he said confidently.

She looked at the clock. "Sir, it's afternoon."

"Well, it was morning when I got here. I was hoping to have a moment of your time."

"Do I have a choice?"

He smiled again. "Unfortunately, I can be fairly persistent, and I don't think my wife would like me coming back after being gone this long without some answers. I assure you, it will only take a few minutes. I'm certain you're a very busy woman."

He doubted she was busy beyond eating her way to retirement. He wasn't going to leave without getting the police report regarding his grandfather's death. He and Callie would never be able to start their lives until they buried the past of Grant Manor once and for all. The chief grunted and jerked her head toward her office. Mike nearly leaped over the gate separating the back rooms from the reception area to follow her inside. She took her time nestling behind the desk.

"What can I help you with, Mr. Grant?" she asked, her tone dripping hostility.

"Well, I see you know who I am. I was looking into my grandfather's passing and was hoping to get a copy of the police report."

"You don't trust our work?"

He grinned. "Of course I do. I'm a writer, though, and I find the story fascinating. Call it morbid curiosity."

"We don't take too kindly to people digging up the past around here," she snapped. "And I don't care what your reasoning is; call it respect for the dead."

"Am I mistaken in the assumption that its public record?" he asked.

"Excuse me?"

"Well now, I don't know much about the law, but I do know in order for a will to be executed, there has to be a death certificate. For that, you'd need a closed case. Now, I'm not presuming to know your job—"

"A wise decision. You've got a lot of nerve showing up here, asking about those poor kids' murder. What, with him being your kin and all, I'd think—"

"Benjamin was no family of mine," Mike growled. "I do

know the law, though, and I've got every right to ask for those records."

She glared at him. "I suppose you do. Unfortunately, out here, we haven't digitized anything yet. It's an old system. It could take months to find them. If you want to leave your number with Carson out front, I'll have him start looking right away."

Mike snorted. He wasn't going to give up that easy. The deaths weren't even a year old. In a town as small as theirs, there was no way the chief didn't know exactly where she'd placed the file. It had to be the only murder in the last decade. Even someone as obviously unmotivated as she was would keep it around. No, she was intentionally making the search for answers difficult. Mike had to wonder what she was hiding or if it was just a general disdain for him as the rest of the town seemed to have. Either way, he wasn't going to let it go.

"Of course," he said courteously. "I'm sure you're swamped with work. If you'd like, I have a detective friend back in New York who would be happy to come down and go through the files…."

"I don't like the tone of your voice," she hissed.

Mike leveled his gaze at hers. "I don't like getting the run-around on things, especially from a woman in a position of power. What happened to your oath to serve and protect? How much protection did you give my grandfather?"

"I think we're done here."

Mike shrugged. "Sure, if that's what you want…but I'll be back tomorrow and the next day, and the next. I'll bring every friend and connection back in New York that I have down to your little community."

"Young man, what do you think you are going to find by looking into this?" she asked.

Mike sighed. "Honestly, I don't know, but I know something is going on at that house, and the way to find out what it is, is to start digging. If that's what I have to spend the next ten years of my life doing, then I'll be here, doing it and using every last penny I have in the process."

"Mister, I think you better check your tone before you go making threats like that. This is a tight-knit community. You don't want to go stirring up any trouble."

"You're absolutely right. I don't want to stir anything up, but I sure as hell will if that's what it takes to get the answers I need. Now, are you going to help with those files, or do I need to call some friends?"

"I told you'd we'd look for them, and I will, just as soon as I've got the manpower."

Mike glared at her and rose. "Then I suggest you find the men really fast. I'm not going to let this go. I'm going to find out what this town is hiding and what really happened to my grandfather. You can either help me in that, or you can try to fight against me, but either way, it's going to happen."

Her glare could cut through glass, but her pursed lips twitched a little. Mike had spent his life watching people. He could tell from her mouth that she wasn't going to keep pushing him, thank God. His actual list of friends in New York was short, and those who could help him wouldn't be inclined to do so. All in all, it was a bluff on his part without question. Thankfully, the ploy seemed to be working.

"I think we might have the file laying around here somewhere," she grumbled.

"Thank you, I can wait while you go get it."

"It's the only copy, and our printer is broken. I can't let you leave with it, and I won't have you taking any pictures. It's still a police report and whatnot. You can stay put. I'll be back once I find it."

Mike nodded but said nothing. He was sure the wait in the lobby was going to be short compared to what he was about to endure. Grabbing his phone as the chief stormed out, he shot a quick text to his wife, not wanting her to worry or come after him. At least he was making progress. He could only hope Callie was fairing the same in her search for answers.

ike swore under his breath when half an hour passed without the woman returning. He had been honest with her when he had said he would wait as long as needed, but he hadn't expected her to actually make him sit around for days on end. After what felt like an eternity, the door finally reopened, and the chief returned. She tossed the file onto the desk. The bloodied crime-scene photos slipping from the folder just enough to catch Mike's attention. He wanted to look away but couldn't. The morbid curiosity pushed him forward.

He tugged out the first photo. It was a gruesome scene from his grandfather's study. The single puncture at the back of his neck had bled profusely. Mike reached around to rub his own neck. The angle was awkward. Why would anyone plunge a blade into the back of their neck to kill themself? It didn't add up with the story he'd been told. Moving the picture aside, he scanned over the actual report quickly, his anger building with each line.

"This says that he killed the children, then himself?" Mike asked.

"If that's what it says, that's how it happened."

"I don't understand why he would stab himself like that. Would he even have the strength to get through the bone?"

"So you're a detective now, too?"

"No, but I'm wondering what sort of show you're running down here if you think he killed himself. It's no wonder you don't want me taking these. Where is the murder weapon?"

"It was never recovered, and it wasn't a murder. Forensics looked things over. It was perfectly plausible for him to drive the weapon into his neck after he used it on the children."

"I don't believe it," Mike snapped. "I want to talk to the officer who was called to the scene."

"That would be the young man out there, and I won't have you reminding him of that traumatic experience. He didn't join the force here to witness a scene like that."

"Then he shouldn't be a cop at all. That's part of the job. As a citizen and as Benjamin Grant's grandson, I demand to speak to the officer who handled the case."

"Fine," she snapped.

Mike didn't care about speaking with the officer. He had everything he needed in the police report. What he did need was time alone to get photos of everything. It was the sort of puzzle Callie could help him solve but not if he couldn't take the evidence back to her. Thankfully, he knew how much the chief enjoyed making him wait around. There was no rush as he carefully took pictures of all twenty pages. It was a struggle to look at the images of the children. He made a mental note to hide them from Callie. There was no point in her suffering more.

He quickly finished the task at hand, tucking his phone back into his pocket just as the door opened. The officer who had been sitting at the desk came in and stood awkwardly as the chief took her place behind the desk again. Mike hadn't planned ahead. He had no idea what to ask the man standing in front of him. His mind started to race through what he'd looked at in the file.

"What made you think it was a suicide?" Mike asked.

"There was no sign of forced entry. The old man had been losing his mind for years, and everyone knew it. He guarded those kids like a lunatic. Everything fit. If he couldn't have them, then no one could. He went off the deep end and took innocent lives in the process. I don't like the kinds of questions you're asking," he growled.

"Well, someone has to ask them because this was obviously sloppy police work—"

The chief cleared her throat. "I won't have you speaking ill of my deputies. He did everything by the book. If you want to look over the file, that's your prerogative, but I won't have you stirring up mud where there isn't any."

"Are you sure about that?" Mike snapped. "Tell me something, what would happen to the property if I weren't around, huh?"

"I assume it would go to the surrounding city," she snarled. "Is that your ploy? Someone offed him for the land? You've got a lot of nerve. The Grant family has been a thorn in this town's side from day one."

"Lady, all I wanted was to get a fresh start, but now it's on my head to find out what really happened to Benjamin. I think it's obvious you have no desire to help me, so I'll take my leave, but I promise, this isn't the last you're going to hear from me. Especially if I find out something nefarious is happening around here."

"You better watch your back, boy," the chief hissed.

"Trust me, I'm not the only one," Mike snapped.

He stood and spun around, jerking open the door and storming out of the building. He had what he came for and so much more. Knowing the local law was somehow involved in the entire mystery did little to ease his anger. If they were going to get help catching the real killer, it would need to come from outside the small community. It was starting to become clear the only person they could trust was Frank and possibly the bank owner. He'd come through on his promise of a loan and seemed excited to share the upcoming news of the Grant Manor Bed and Breakfast. Most of the community still seemed downright horrified that the home hadn't been demolished after the deaths that had happened there.

Mike gunned the engine of his pickup and flew out of town. He didn't slow down again until turning on the gravel road that led home. His phone had half a dozen texts on it from Callie, but he was too angry to stop to reply. When he reached the manor, Mike took several deep breaths before climbing out. Callie would already be upset over his hostile reception at the police station. His anger would do nothing but escalate the situation. Armed with the photos, Mike jumped out and smiled the instant Lizzy darted into his arms. How could he not fight for such a beautiful little girl? His heart wrenched, thinking of her ghostly playmate. He hugged her a little tighter as she told him about her afternoon.

Callie met the duo on the porch. He smiled at her as she handed him a cold beer. The woman knew him well. It was sweltering out, and the station had no air conditioning. The heat had undoubtedly helped fuel his irritation over the situation. Lizzy was gone, off playing at the lake, as quickly as she'd appeared. The couple sat in silence for a few minutes. Mike drank his beer while Callie sipped on iced tea. Had it not been for the weight of Benjamin and the twins, it would have been a perfect afternoon. All Mike wanted was a dozen more just like it, minus the hauntings. Callie let out a content sigh before dropping one of Benjamin's journals on the wicker table.

"So, it's been an interesting morning. How did it go for you?" Callie asked.

He groaned. "I'm really starting to hate this town. I've got pictures of the case file, but the witch of a chief wouldn't make me a copy. I'm lucky I even snuck the photos. Let me tell you, if I didn't already think something was up, that little visit with the chief would have definitely convinced me. They're all hiding something around here."

"Well, that makes sense. Frank told me the whole town thought Benjamin had something to do with Mae and

Maria's disappearances, too. The neighbor didn't think very fondly of him or his family, either."

"You mean *my* family?" Mike grumbled.

"Oh, stop it, you are nothing like him, I can promise you that. I don't know, though. Benjamin only ever spoke with love for Mae. I don't see him being the monster everyone makes him out to be."

"He was no saint," Mike replied. "Don't forget I've felt the man's anger a few times now. He wasn't the type to make friends."

"But do you really think he was a serial killer?" Callie asked.

Mike paused to think for a moment. It was a question he'd already asked himself a dozen times. His grandfather had been angry and held some deeply rooted, distorted values, but he'd never come across as a murderer. When the spirit had taken hold of his body, the only time there had been any affection or tenderness from the restless spirit had been when the children played through his mind. Mike shook his head.

"No. Benjamin Grant was no killer. He was framed."

33

*B*y the time they were done swapping information, the sun was setting in the sky. Mike felt fatigued. Callie picked up on her husband's weighted mind instantly. Despite his protest, Callie convinced him to take one of her sleeping pills. It was a hard choice to make, but Benjamin's using his body had taken its toll on him. The restless dreams he'd been having no longer felt like they were empty threats. Work done, Mike relented and willingly took the small pill before lying down. Callie, his wonderful Callie, had already put Lizzy to bed and read her a story. He slipped off into blissful sleep.

Mike's eyes flew open. The air in the room felt stagnant, covering the space in a film of haze. Callie slept peacefully next to him as he climbed out of bed quietly. Despite the aged bed, there was no noise when he moved. It was strange, given the frame's tendency to creak with every movement. The warm air was off. His eyes darted around the room as his heart started to race. It had only been a few seconds, but Mike was quick to realize he was trapped in a dream. Beyond the bedroom door, the hallway light glowed, a soft scratching now working its way through the silence. He couldn't place the noise, but it felt familiar, almost soothing to him. Determined to find the source, he moved past the bedroom and down the hall to the staircase.

At the top of the steps, he turned toward Lizzy's room but instantly felt unease. The dream didn't want him to stray off its given course. Pulling his attention away from the instinct to check on his daughter, he slowly stepped closer to the study. The instant he pushed open the door, the noise stopped. His grandfather looked up at him, a scowl moving across his wrinkled face as he took in his grandson's disheveled appearance. He jerked his head toward the free chair. Mike instantly sat across from the ghostly figure.

"Fucking idiot detective I hired to find you missed the kid," Benjamin growled.

"I...I don't understand," Mike stammered, his voice sounding distant. "Do you know who killed you?"

"That doesn't matter. None of that does. You need to leave. Get your kid out of here."

"The detective..." Mike muttered. "...kid...you didn't know that I had a daughter, did you? So what, you were happy to let whatever evil spirit loose on me but not her?"

"You are just like your father," he hissed. "He never listened, either. Get your wife, your daughter, and get the hell out of my house."

"No! I need to know what happened to you!" Mike yelled.

The figure scowled at him again before seeming to look through Mike. He shot back daggers, taking a moment to look at him in detail. He was too stunned to notice the trickle of blood slowly moving down the right breast pocket of Benjamin's pressed shirt. Benjamin didn't answer him. The spirit rubbed his eyes, trying to focus his gaze on the journal in front of him as he picked up his quill. The noise returned. Mike's head was spinning. He now understood that he was watching the man die all over again. He wasn't frantically racing for the door as he'd done in reality, but the blood pooled on his lap as the scratching became erratic. He watched in stunned horror as his grandfather slumped over the desk, the room filling with a foreboding silence.

Mike stood up, the chair behind him falling to the floor without making a sound as he backed away from the scene in panic. He grabbed the door and jerked it open, running down the hall to the steps. He was just about to force himself awake when a familiar giggle came from the room that belonged to Lizzy. Mike's stomach plunged. Changing directions, he stepped carefully to the cracked bedroom door and peeked in. His daughter slept peacefully in her bed. Her rhythmic breathing brought him comfort. Nausea coursed through him as he connected the dots and realized why the child's laughter had sounded so familiar. It was the same one he'd heard the night Lizzy had hidden in the kitchen cubby. His eyes darted around the room, landing on the small figures sitting near the window.

He wanted to look away from the two children. The image almost made him vomit. Vera was on her knees, brushing Marcus's hair as he played with two toy soldiers. The scene would be perfectly loving in another setting. Mike couldn't look away from their necks, though. Vera whispered something to Marcus, making the little boy giggle with delight. They were blissfully unaware of the gaping wounds in their skin. Cuts so deep no one could survive them. A devastated sob escaped Mike's lips. The figures froze instantly, both looking in his direction. At first, they seemed pleased by his presence, but it quickly turned to matching looks of horror. Mike realized he was going to see their deaths happen, just as he had with Benjamin.

He closed his eyes as the children's pleas filled the air, only drown out by his own screams.

CALLIE HAD BEEN EXHAUSTED all afternoon. The emotional and physical toll that living in a manor had on a person had started to catch up with her. She didn't need any pills to help her sleep. The second Lizzy collapsed into bed next to Mike, she started snoring. No sooner had she closed her eyes than the world around her slipped away. Callie found herself sitting on the porch swing once again, the warm sun perfectly kissing her skin as the breeze toyed with the hem of her sundress. She could hear Mike and Gavin working inside. Lizzy was down by the lake, playing tag with her friends. The moment was beautifully serene, broken only by Lizzy calling for her.

She rose and ambled to the edge of the porch as the two girls and boy ran up to her. All three wore matching smiles. Something had them excited. Their childish delight was infectious. Callie smiled and happily followed after them to the lake to see what they'd found. Maria had set up a few fishing traps near the edge. With the perfect weather, she and Mae wanted to do a fish fry over the weekend. Callie's stomach growled as she remembered the smell of deep-fried fish, Mae's special recipe.

"What did you guys find?" Callie asked the trio.

They moved aside so she could see, but none of them picked up the object. Clouds started to move in, giving Callie a chill as she approached. The knife was muddy. She picked it up and started cleaning it off with her dress. It was like nothing she'd ever seen. Obviously, it was an antique, but how it had gotten there, she couldn't fathom. The weapon was made of solid gold with four sharp edges that formed a cross all the way up to the ornately deco-rated handle. She ran her finger along the blade, a sharp pain shooting through her body as she jerked back her finger. A droplet of blood appeared on the blade for a split second before disappearing again. Callie dropped the knife. Her eyes darted to Lizzy, who now stood alone a few feet from her.

"Where are the others?" Callie asked.

Lizzy sobbed. "Mommy, why are you doing this?"

"What, honey? What's wrong?" she frantically asked.

The girl screamed and darted away when Callie reached for her. She looked down to see what had scared her daughter. Her dress was covered in blood, a stab wound bleeding profusely in the center of her abdomen. She pressed her hand against it, trying to slow the bleeding. Beneath her fingers, the crossed blade had been plunged completely through.

34

*C*allie plunged her fingers into the flowerbeds, forming a gap in the soft earth before planting another bundle of flowers. She'd never been much for gardening, but the cool breeze and bright sun made the job peaceful. As she worked and watched Lizzy play with the sitter she'd hired that morning, she sang softly under her breath. The eerie tune was ingrained in her mind after hearing it the night before in her dream. She knew the song held some significance, but she could tell what it was yet. Her mind played the dream again as she searched for clues.

He paid sixpence for his bride so pure,
Though all the men desired her.
She loved him well for all her life,
And was forever a docile wife.
But her family's curse persisted still,
Despite her name dropped from the will.

The Perry fortune mattered scant,
To the heiress maiden who became a Grant.

The song died on her lips as Lizzy squealed with delight near the water's edge. Callie watched the two play for a few minutes. The girl was barely eighteen. She was a friend of Gavin's who was home for the summer from college. After checking her references and grilling the poor girl for an hour, Callie had joyfully brought her on board as a staff member.

Knowing Lizzy had someone to watch her constantly gave Callie the time she needed to keep pursuing her research. Mike and Gavin appeared on the porch a short time later. She met them at the swing and gratefully took the glass of water her husband offered. Things were progressing inside. Gavin had already made half a dozen trips to the hardware and was headed out for another.

Mike sat down beside his wife when Gavin left. The serene landscape held them both in captive silence for a few minutes. They'd already talked about everything going on, including the dreams. Had the house not needed their attention, they'd have already parted ways to continue the search for answers. As it was, Mike had a little work to finish up, and Callie wanted to make sure the new sitter, Gale, was a good fit for Lizzy before leaving her alone. Later, they'd head to town to follow up on a few leads.

"Did I tell you I'm going to reach out to Chuck?" Mike asked.

"You're old college roommate? Isn't he working for Sampson and Sons now?"

Mike nodded. "They mostly do real estate law, but I want him to look over the police report for me. There is no way it was a suicide, and I think he'll agree."

"Good, well, while you're doing that, I'm going to go to the grocery store. Not that I don't love having you do all the shopping...."

He grinned. "I'll be happy to hand the reins back to you."

Callie looked past him. He turned to see Frank walking slowly up the steps as he watched the teen and girl playing in the yard. After a few more steps, he turned to the couple, who insisted he sit down and join them. Callie wanted to know more about Benjamin, but Frank always seemed to talk in riddles. Hopefully, if he understood they didn't believe his friend had committed suicide, the elderly man would be more inclined to help them find the real killer.

"I was hoping we'd be able to talk for a few minutes. I didn't want to bother you at your cabin, though," Callie said.

"I appreciate that, ma'am. Even Benjamin made sure to give me my space. A man needs room," he added.

"Of course, now that you're here, would you mind telling us about Benjamin a little?"

He stiffened. "I don't think it's right to talk about the dead."

"I understand, but it would really help us in figuring out this house. There is something not quite right about the police report," Mike said.

"You saw that?" he asked.

The couple nodded.

Frank's jaw clenched. "Benjamin was a good man. A little rough around the edges, for sure, but that's just how you were raised back in the day. His mind turned on him, though, not long after the kids were born. He was sure those twins were a bad omen."

"Really?" Callie stammered. "It didn't seem like that to me."

"You didn't know him like I did. Things got worse after Maria died, but even before that, he'd tell me the twins were out to get his money. They were evil, even. He went mad. I think the two of you are just looking to cook up trouble."

"No," Mike cautioned. "It's nothing like that. We just want to know what happened to my grandfather. Callie has been reading his journals. There is no question he had a few screws loose there at the end, but there is no way he could have stabbed himself in that position. It just doesn't make any sense."

"That cop that came out here might have rushed through things, but he did a fine job. I'll stand by his work. Benjamin had his enemies, but no one out there would want him dead, not even Collin after all that legal business."

"What business?" Callie asked.

"That little shit went and tried to sue Benjamin for the property. He said your grandfather was holding up progress. Of course, he didn't expect old Ben to bring in some friends. The poor attorney Collin hired was eaten alive in there. Been bad blood between the two ever since, but even he wouldn't do something like you're talking about. Those two kids were murdered. That's not something a sane man does."

"Well, the promise of money does a lot of things to men. I'm sure you know that. The property wouldn't have ever gone to Collin, though, not for a very long time."

"I don't think he'd do something like this, known the boy my whole life. No, Maria, Mae, the twins, all of them were tied to Benjamin. I couldn't ever prove it, but he wasn't ever in his right mind, not as long as I knew him. You two can keep digging all you want, but all you're going to stir up is trouble."

"Frank, if I didn't know you better, I'd say that sounded like a threat," Mike joked.

Frank chuckled. "I just want you two to be safe. You're the last of the Grants. Shame if something happened to you two."

"Well, if there's a killer out there, I'd be worried, too. Are you sure you don't know anyone who would do something like this?" Callie asked.

"I've already told you, Benjamin did this. He may have looked like a loving grandfather to those two, but behind closed doors, he hated them. I'd venture to say he despised them. He saw a darkness in them that I can't even describe. Now tell me, does that sound like a sane man or a murderer? You need to let it go."

Callie sighed and stood up. She couldn't sit there and listen to Frank any longer. It was infuriating to know he didn't believe them. As Benjamin's best friend, it only seemed right that he'd want his friend to be remembered as a victim and not a killer. Storming down the steps, she went back to her gardening. She could still hear the two men but quickly started to drown them out when they began talking about the house's foundation inspection. There was nothing left to interest her. She started to hum the song from her dream again. For whatever reason, the morbid tune made her feel at ease.

"You all right there, Frank?" Mike asked.

Callie looked up and tumbled back onto her rear in shock. The man had moved to the edge of the porch, standing just a few feet above her with a look of pure terror in his eyes. All color had drained from his face. Callie could see his aged knuckles whitening under the grip he had on the railing. Yet his eyes were what terrified her the most. They seemed to look right through her, a rage behind them she couldn't comprehend.

"Where did you hear that?" he hissed.

Callie swallowed. "It was in one of Benjamin's journals."

"You're lying. You didn't hear a song like that in a journal. How did you know the tune?" he growled.

Callie swallowed. "I was just guessing at it. Why? Does it mean something to you?"

"Of course not," he croaked.

The lie was a small one, but she didn't think he'd believe the truth. If he wasn't going to help them find out what happened, though, she wasn't going to share information with him willingly. Frank swallowed, snapping himself out of the trance before turning and storming off the porch in the direction of his cabin. Callie sat, looking at her husband in stunned shock.

"What the hell was that all about?" Mike asked.

Callie shook her head, unable to answer.

5

"*W*hat the hell was that about?" Mike stammered.

Callie's mouth hung open in shock. She had no idea what had set him off.

"I don't know. That was weird, though. He sure didn't seem to like that song," Callie muttered.

"It didn't sound like he was very fond of Collin, either. I guess I didn't put together what a small town this is. Collin never mentioned he'd had troubles with my grandfather."

"Well, that's something you two have in common then, keeping secrets," Callie replied. "I'd forgotten about it with everything going on, but you didn't tell me I wasn't on the deed or the loan for that matter."

"Whoa, what are you talking about?" Mike asked. "We did the power of attorney. You know you're on it!"

"Oh really?" Callie asked.

218

Mike glared at her and stormed inside. He reappeared a few minutes later with an opened manila folder in his hands. He was scanning the pages quickly before moving on to the next one. She waited for him to give her some proof. The shock and hurt in his eyes had been genuine. Callie wondered if she'd made a huge mistake in confronting him. Mike grabbed the paperwork and flipped it back to the beginning, looking through everything for a second time before meeting Callie's gaze in shock. He shook his head.

"Callie, I swear to you, I swear on Lizzy's life—"

"It's not in there, is it? The land and loan are all in your name."

"I...I don't know what happened. Collin took everything to make copies. We talked about the loan. He even said it had to be in your name, but it's right here, in mine. I...I don't know what to say."

"It's okay. I don't think you had anything to do with it. I'm sorry I snapped at you."

"Don't be! Oh my God, please don't be sorry. This is my fault. I should have looked over everything a second time in his office. I'm going down there right now to find out what the hell is going on and to get you on the paperwork. How did you know to look?"

"It was something the woman next door said to me," Callie replied. "Why would Collin do that? It's like he only wanted it in your name? Do you think he's like your grandfather and thinks women shouldn't hold property?"

"I don't know, but I'm going to go find out. I don't take

lightly to having the wool pulled over my eyes. Plus, he wasn't exactly forthcoming about his relationship with my grandfather. I'm going to go get some answers."

"Well, for starters, if the loan is only in your name and you used the property to get the loan, wouldn't it go to the bank if something happened to you?"

"No, not with the last page of the deed that you found. He doesn't know that, though. He probably thinks the whole thing will default to him. My God, Callie, do you know what that means? He probably thought the bank would get the property after my grandfather died, too. Think about it. Without that last page, it would go up at auction, and he's about the only big fish in town."

Callie gasped. "He's the one who killed your grandfather!"

"We need to get ahold of the law and fast. I'm going to go send all of this to Chuck and see what he thinks. If he says there is enough to open a case, he'll have the law altered, and I'll make sure he knows it better not be the local ones, either. I know they have something to do with this, too."

"Well, it fits together. If Collin gets the property, the town would be booming with lake tourism. The state would give the police more money to operate, and that chief would get a big fat bonus."

"It's no wonder this town hates us. Who knows how many of them are in on this. I'm going to have a few words with Collin," Mike growled.

Callie's stomach rolled. She didn't like the idea of her

husband going to meet with the man who may have killed an old man and two innocent children. Who knew what he was really capable of.

"I know that look," Mike said with a grin. "I'm not going to outright accuse him of anything, okay? I just want to know what the hell he knows about this land and why your name isn't on the paperwork."

"Promise me you won't do anything until we hear back from Chuck?"

"I promise, sweetheart. I wouldn't put you and Lizzy at risk like that. Are you going to be okay here, or do you want to ride into town with me?"

"I'm going to see what else I can learn from Benjamin's study after I get this flowerbed done. I trust Gale. I just think we've learned so much from Benjamin already. I need to focus my attention on the house and the answers it might have. Maybe we'll get lucky and the ghosts will lead me to the murder weapon."

Mike cringed. "I'd forgotten about that. Promise me you'll be safe, too?"

"I will," Callie said as she rose.

She met her husband at the bottom of the steps for a tender embrace before watching him leave. After peeking around the corner to see Gale and Lizzy wading in the water, Callie dropped to her knees again to finish the rest of the front beds before heading inside for a few hours. Gale was with them until six and already had picnic plans for the pair's lunch. She dove back into the task at hand, jerking free a hearty vine working its way up the lattice.

The loose mulch on the ground gave way as she tugged, revealing a black wire. The shape made Callie jump. At first, she'd thought it was a black snake. She continued to tug on it, crawling on her knees along the porch's lattice to where it turned.

Her hand trembled when she saw the camera. Despite its dirty surrounding, it looked to be in pristine shape. It was placed facing the driveway and right where she'd been gardening earlier. Had it not been for the glowing red light, indicating it was still being fed power, Callie wouldn't have been concerned. She quickly darted her eyes away from it, covering the wire back up as she moved away. The line stopped at the other end of the house, seemingly buried somewhere under the plush grass. Her mind was still on the light. Frank hadn't mentioned the cameras and didn't seem to know anything about them, yet someone had buried the line long ago.

If it were still being streamed and fed somewhere, it had to be close by. Callie called out to Gale and headed into the house to start searching. The most logical place would be in Benjamin's study. For the first time since she had arrived, Callie didn't go directly to the desk and start reading his journals. Instead, she ran her hands along the books again, searching for a laptop or missed television somewhere. Along the opposite wall, Callie pulled back a heavy curtain and found a flat-screen built into the wall. It was small and outdated but jumped to life the instant she switched it on. The yard came into view. She let out a breath of relief. It was still up and running, but better yet, the feed was safely in the office and not being streamed to some unknown location.

Grabbing the television's remote off a dusty shelf, she started to rewind the footage, anxious to see how long the record would go back. She watched herself talking with Mike, then Frank appeared on the porch. Her hand trembled when a shadow caught her eye. Slowing down the rewind, Callie watched in horror as two figures appeared behind her image on the screen. Mike was still sitting out of view on the porch swing, but the look on Frank's face suddenly made perfect sense. The slender silhouettes ran to two sets of feet. The matching paint on their toes made Callie's blood run cold. She darted back to Benjamin's desk and grabbed the framed picture of Mae and Maria. Their bare feet were buried in the Lakes sand with nothing more than painted toes sticking through.

She looked back to the frozen image on the screen. A pool of water beneath the decaying flesh of the two women made her queasy. The two had never left the estate. No. They were still in the water. Her stomach lurched. The same water Lizzy was playing in. Instantly, she bolted from her chair and down the steps, nearly colliding with Gale and Lizzy on the steps. She struggled to catch her breath.

"Stay out of the water, okay?" Callie stammered.

Gale looked terrified. "Okay, is everything all right?"

Callie nodded. "Yeah, we might have bacteria. I just want to play it safe."

"Sure, no problem. We were done anyway. You ready to go pack our picnic?" Gale asked Lizzy.

She nodded, hugging her mom before following after Gale. The young girl still looked shaken, but it was better she not know the truth. Not until Callie was sure it was safe.

ike didn't have to wait long once he got to the bank. Collin seemed genuinely thrilled to see his most recent big client there twice in one week. Once Collin saw Mike's demeanor, though, it became obvious that he was concerned. He quickly ushered Mike into his office and closed the door. The man looked nervous for the first time as he offered Mike a drink. Mike declined, keeping his gaze leveled on Collin as he tossed the manila folder onto the desk. While he'd driven into town, Mike had come up with a plan.

"Is everything okay with the loan?" Collin asked. "If you think you need more, I'm sure we could work something out."

"Actually, the house is becoming something of a problem. Or rather, my wife is. She keeps seeing me sinking her money into it and is starting to get fired up."

Collin chuckled, easing some. "Well, that's women for

you. They want to have control of everything. I wouldn't worry too much about it. I'm sure she'll come around."

"Honestly, I'm tired of fighting with her at this point. She wants to have her own debit card for the account, wants all the paperwork, too, so she can keep her own records. I figured since she's on there with me, why not just make her happy?"

Collin swallowed. "Sure thing! You know I'd be happy to set you up with our bank accountant. I can give you her email and phone number that way your wife can reach out—"

"I think it would be best just to do things her way."

"Of course," he muttered. "Of course. Now, getting a bank card will take about a week or so, but I'll get it ordered right away."

"That's fine. I'll just take the bank statements and whatnot right now, then. Maybe that will placate her for a few days anyway."

Collin's eye twitched as he smiled. "Of course, we're a little backed up right now, but if you come back in a few hours, I'll have those ready for you."

"That's fine. I'll wait."

"I'm sorry, Mr. Grant, but I've got another customer coming in for an appointment soon. I'll give you a call when they are ready."

"I'll wait in the lobby then. I sat at the police precinct for almost three hours to get the copies of my grandfather's case report; I don't mind waiting for this as well."

He snorted. "I doubt you got a copy of that."

Mike pulled out his phone and showed Collin the

picture he'd taken of the crime scene. The man gagged visibly. Despite his reaction, Mike's heart sank. It was apparent he didn't have the stomach to carry out his plan alone. His mind started to race. Was the chief helping him? It fit together perfectly. The woman hadn't been forthcoming whatsoever. Mike questioned his decision to come into the bank. If the two were working together, he might have just spurned them to take more action.

"I have had enough," Collin snapped as he jumped from his chair. "I don't know what you're playing at, but you've got no right to come in here and show me a picture like that! You're playing some sort of sick game here, aren't you?"

"I assure you, the only playing games here is you. I want those papers, and I want to know why the hell my wife's name isn't on them. What's your angle?"

"I don't know what you're talking about, but I will not be spoken to like this in my own bank. I think you need to leave."

"Screw what you want. Why did you do it?" Mike hissed.

"You know what? I've had just about enough. I don't think we are going to offer you the same line of credit, after all, Mr. Grant."

"Do whatever the fuck you want," he snapped. "I don't need your goddamn blood money to make that place something, and you better believe I'm going to get to the bottom of all this. You and that sheriff better watch your backs."

"That's it, I'm calling the police," he snarled.

"Go ahead! She's on your fucking payroll, too, isn't she? Is she the one who killed him?"

Someone knocked on the door, breaking the tension in the room. An elderly security guard poked his head into the office and took in the scene before stepping the rest of the way inside. His hand rested on a taser strapped to his side. Mike shot Collin one final look before snatching the file off his desk again and heading for the door.

"This isn't over," he snarled.

"You can go to hell, you and all the other Grants. That place should be burned to the ground," Collin snapped back.

Mike fought the urge to lunge for him. It was exactly what Collin wanted. If Mike were locked away in jail for assault, he would be causing them significantly less trouble. He was done with Collin anyway. The man had sealed his fate. Storming out of the bank, Mike went immediately to the library and printed off the images on his phone. That, along with the loan information, would be enough to get Chuck started, but he still wanted a copy of the deed and final page before sending it off. He gunned his truck the quarter-mile down the road, stopping at the attorney's office.

Thankfully, the old man didn't give him any trouble. He was happy to hand over a copy of everything just as long as it would get Mike away from him again. All he wanted to do was be left alone to watch his programs in the chilled air-conditioning of his office. With the last of the paperwork gathered up, Mike speed out of town in the direction of the manor. He didn't slow down when the police cruiser pulled out behind him and when it flashed its light halfway down the deserted road the manor sat on, he gunned the engine. There was no way in hell he'd be alone in the middle of nowhere with the crooked chief.

He peeled into the driveway, grateful to see Gavin and Frank both outside the house. They were hanging a ladder to start cleaning out the house's gutters when he threw his truck into park and climbed out, slamming the door before storming to the cruiser. The rage inside of him felt familiar, like Benjamin Grant had returned, but Mike knew the fury was all his own. All he'd wanted was to have a peaceful life with his wife and daughter. Instead, he was living in a circus.

The woman stepped out and started shouting at Mike. "I have half a mind to arrest you for fleeing!"

"I didn't know you were following me, and you'll have a hard time proving that in a court of law. If I was speeding, go ahead and give me a ticket, but I'd rather have witnesses here."

"I don't know what you're plan is by stirring up everyone in my town, boy, but I've just about had it. I got a call from that fella over at the bank saying you showed him crime scene photos?"

"You've got some nerve," Mike hissed.

Callie and Lizzy appeared on the porch. The little girl ran to her father before he could stop her. Mike picked her up, whispering a greeting before putting her back down. He was struggling to keep his head on straight. Frank and Gavin were approaching the pair now.

"Afternoon, Sheriff," Frank said casually. "Everything okay?"

"Your new friend here has been causing all sorts of problems," she snapped. "He about gave Al over at the bank a heart attack."

Frank chuckled. "Hell, Sheriff, Al's so damn old he probably gets one just standing up. You know these young 'uns have been under a lot of pressure, trying to make this place nice again. I'm sure he didn't mean anything by it. Why don't you go on and check on old Al? I'll handle Mr. Grant here."

Her eyes flickered away from Mike to Frank. She pursed her lips but gave a curt nod. "You best talk some sense into him, Frank. Otherwise, I'll be tossing him in the slammer before long."

"Boy," Frank said after a low whistle, "I don't know what you did to ruffle that old hag's feathers, but I sure wouldn't be going back into town any time soon. You sure did get under her skin."

"Yeah, well, the feeling is mutual."

"Son, I think it's about time you let all this go. You've got a family to think about here. What would your grand-father think of all this?" Frank asked.

Mike bit his tongue to keep quiet as the sheriff climbed back into her car and sped away. He let out the breath he was holding until the dust from her tires ended at the main road, where it turned to blacktop. Callie ran to his side. He wrapped his arm around her, but he was still shaking. They had to move fast, or they'd be joining Benjamin soon.

*M*ike was only there for a few minutes. He grabbed what he needed and promised to fill in Callie as soon as he returned from mailing the documents to Chuck. Thankfully, Frank was there to watch over the house and Gavin's work so Callie could keep digging. Gale had been more than happy to stay on a few extra hours after learning about the mystery surrounding the family. She had a strange fascination with the supernatural, but Callie wasn't going to judge her for it. At least not after everything Callie had seen recently. With the commotion dying down, she made her way back up the steps. Instantly, she noticed the open attic door.

Callie moved slowly to the hatch. Neither she nor Mike had needed to access it yet. The electricians were still working on the main floor. Not even on their first visit had they considered going up into the unused space. She tugged on the cord, and the steps unfurled in front of her. A lump rose in her throat. There were two sets of bare footprints on the otherwise dusty steps. They were much too small to belong to an adult. Had they matched, they may have been Lizzy on another exploration, but one set was definitely bigger. Callie climbed the steps slowly, fumbling with the light at the top before it flickered to life. With just her head and shoulders in the space, the dust tingled her nose.

As soon as the light hit the corners of the attic, Callie gasped. Sitting in a rocking chair near the small front window was Benjamin Grant. The chair was there, but the trio of spirits continued to waver in and out of existence. They didn't seem aware of her presence there. Benjamin's gaze was trained on the two children playing on the floor in front of him. They each had a stack of cards. She watched for a few seconds and quickly realized they were playing war. Benjamin would laugh and encourage them each time one or the other won. Callie knew she was witnessing a happy moment for the family. Frank had no idea what he was talking about. Benjamin Grant loved Vera and Marcus both.

Callie's nose tingled again. This time she couldn't stifle the sneeze. Opening her eyes, Callie found all three spirits staring at her. She swallowed, trying not to move. It didn't matter that she knew they were trying to help her solve the case. The very reality that such things existed was sitting just feet away from her, not looking through her but at her. Her body was trembling. It was impossible not to be shaken. Vera crawled in her direction, a welcoming smile on her face as Marcus followed after her. Benjamin called the children back but neither listened. They obviously didn't feel threatened by their loving caregiver.

"You have to find it, you know," Vera whispered. "You have to. She said you could!"

"Find what?" Callie stammered. "We know it was Collin. We are trying to get him brought to justice. I promise you."

"Kids," Benjamin grumbled. "Get back here."

"Please, please help us. Find it. You have to help us!" Vera stammered. "We're running out of time. You're going to be here with us forever soon, too."

Callie's heart raced. "What do you mean?"

Her head was racing as she tried to piece together the child's words. Dull pain in her abdomen reminded her of the dream the night before. She could almost feel the blade digging into her flesh. She shuddered. They had to be looking for the murder weapon. If she could find it, there would be fingerprints. Callie was certain she'd find someone else's besides Benjamin's on it. The little girl's face turned to a look of horror as she gazed past Callie. She spun around to see what Vera was looking at, but there was nothing in the attic but them and a few moth-eaten boxes.

"Who is it, Vera?" she asked. "Who did this to you? Just give me a name!"

"Pawpaw tells us not to be afraid of them, but I can't help it. I just can't," the girl sobbed. "Please help us and the others."

"What others?"

Vera jerked her head. Callie turned to look for a

second time. The image that greeted her nearly knocked her off the steep ladder. Inches from her head lay a body. The sound of dripping water broke the silence; it was coming from the corpse. Vera had shrunk away from Callie again, and she could understand why. The disfigured body was bloated with little pieces of decaying flesh chewed away. As if the image weren't poignant enough, it was the smell that made Callie fight back vomit. The sour taste filled her nostrils. She'd smelled it before, years ago as a little girl, near her grandparents' lake house. Instantly, the memory came flooding back to her.

Despite her grandmother insisting Callie stay near the house, she'd been curious from a young age, much like Lizzy. Her grandparents had barely stepped inside when she set off for the woods. Callie had been determined to prove to her grandfather that she could check the traps on her own. At seven years old, she knew better than to touch them, even if a rabbit or raccoon was inside. He'd promised her all summer that by the end of the season, she'd be able to do it herself. With just a few days of vacation left, though, Callie had given up on her grandfather's keeping his promise. She was too young to understand he was protecting her, too impatient to sit and listen when the elders spoke. Instead, she tromped off, unaware that a rabid wolf had attacked a hiker in the area.

A few minutes later, Callie found herself face to face with the same wolf. Her scream pierced the trees. It sent the wolf running and her grandfather racing to her rescue. The lengthy talk that came later after a hunting party had put the animal down was one she'd never forget. Ever since, she listened before acting and thought her decisions through. Unfortunately, it wasn't the end of things. On her last day with her grandparents, the loving man had kept his promise. With a watchful eye, he sat on the porch as she bounded off to check the traps for a second time. The hiker's corpse was face down in the river. His punctured lungs snagged on the second trap they'd set days before. The following summer, her grandparents sold the property, and Callie never returned.

Yet the sight and smell of a waterlogged body remained with her forever. It would keep her up at night after a particularly rough day at the hospital. She could still feel the bloated flesh beneath her toes, the way his engorged fingers protruded through the thick mud.

Callie sucked in a sharp breath, a scream rising as she stumbled on the step. Behind her, Vera was screaming for Callie to help them. Tunnel vision closed in. The body was that of Maria, the poor children's mother. She couldn't move. Frozen in fear, she watched the body's throat contract and move as a water snake slipped from between Maria's gray lips. The harmless native creatures weren't venomous but were known for their nasty tempers. It locked eyes with Callie for a split second before lunging. She screamed, losing her footing on the steep incline and tumbling backward off the ladder. A prickling sensation shot through her head as the world around her faded to black.

* * *

"CALLIE!" Gale called. "Wake up! Hey!"

Callie groaned and opened her eyes. Her head felt like it had been split open. Lizzy came into focus. Tears streaked the little girl's face as she clung to her favorite stuffed animal. The instant she saw her mother sit up, she was in her arms. Callie held on to her daughter tightly. She tried to pull her legs underneath herself but a sharp pain shot through her ankle, grabbing her attention. She looked down and saw the two puncture wounds on her upper thigh.

"Whoa, looks like you got bit by something. Are you okay? Girl, you scared the crap out of us. Should we call 9-1-1?" Gale asked.

Callie shook her head. "No, it's fine. I think it was a snake. If it were poisonous, I'd already be feeling the effects of it. It just hurts like a son of a bi...like heck. It must have been in the attic."

"That's an odd place for a snake to live," Gale muttered.

"Trust me, this is an odd house altogether. I must have knocked myself out when I fell off the ladder. Is everything all right with you two?"

Gale nodded. "Yeah, we were about ready to take off with our picnic when we heard you fall. It's a good thing we were still inside. I hate to think of you lying here unconscious for hours. Are you sure we don't need to take you into town?"

"No, I'm fine. You two go and enjoy your picnic, just be safe, okay?"

"Hey, that goes both ways. Maybe no more ladders without a spotter?" Gale said with a grin.

Callie laughed and gave Lizzy one last kiss after promising her daughter that she would be fine. The two helped Callie get to her feet and into the kitchen so she could bandage herself. The pain was already starting to dull in both her thigh and her head. With the attic door safely closed and latched, she sat down and took a deep breath. She was starting to question her resolve. Water snakes didn't live in attics at all.

With the girls happy and safely away from the house, Callie wasn't going to stop pushing for answers. She let herself rest for a few minutes before taking a couple Tylenol and limping her way back upstairs to Benjamin's study. She sat behind the wide desk and tapped her fingers. Whether it was the concussion or insanity setting in, Callie couldn't seem to stay focused. She watched her hands move independently from her mind. The quill felt familiar in her hand. Somehow she knew a blank journal was kept in the center drawer of the desk. Sliding it open, she pulled it out and pressed open the first page. A slightly acidic smell wafted from her right side as the well was uncovered. She dipped in the pen with seasoned expertise despite never having used the tool before.

I don't know where to begin. We know Collin was involved, or so we assume. He couldn't have acted alone, though. I'm almost certain now that Maria and Mae were both murdered

*here on the property as well, but I can't understand why.
Benjamin eluded to some connection between Mae and Frank.
Maybe he introduced her to someone? I know the sheriff seems
to be familiar with everyone. She certainly is old enough to have
been close with Frank and Mae. Was it a love triangle gone
wrong?*

*Did Maria find out about the sheriff killing her mother and
she offed her in the same manner? That would explain why
Frank was able to talk her down so easily. The poor man probably had no idea what she did to Mae. I need to find out more,
but if the sheriff and Collin are working together, we'll need all
the help we can get, including Frank. Hopefully, he's still got
some sharp wits about him.*

Callie put down the quill and grabbed the last journal
she'd been reading. Before long, she was engrossed in
Benjamin's colorful writing once again. This time she was
on a mission, though. His journals made no mention of
the sheriff except for the occasional angry encounter.
There didn't seem to be any relationship between her and
Frank. At least not one that Benjamin knew about. Given
how close the two men were, Callie knew he'd have
shared it. She pressed on when Maria's name caught her
eye a few pages later.

*It seems the boy has some sort of genetic problem. Not that
I'm surprised. He's a sweet kid but always has been a little on
the weak side. Maria has taken it upon herself to trace back her
lineage and find out about any other problems he might be
prone to. I told her the whole thing was hogwash, but she's a
young mother. There is no talking sense into a woman when
their child is sick. For now, the boy just can't rough-house too*

much, something about his blood. It does present a bit of a problem, though.

She's been asking about her father, a secret I promised to take to the grave. Frank has no recollection of that night, and Mae never forgave herself after that. Neither of them was at their best. That's what good drink does to a person...but Frank's had his medical issues. I don't think Mae would want her grandbaby suffering through some of his ailments if it could be helped. She might be rolling in her grave or kick my ass on the other side, but I think I have to tell the girl who her father is.

Callie's mouth hung open as she read the entry for a second time. It was no wonder Frank loved the twins so much. He was their grandfather! The entry was one of the last in the journal. It was infuriating not to know what Frank's reaction had been, though it did help in understanding his eccentric behavior. His entire family had been murdered in a house he despised. Anyone could sympathize with his reasoning that the place was evil. Everything fit together perfectly. Frank was loved by the community. If he swore the place was haunted, then they'd all believe him without question.

It still didn't answer how the sheriff played into everything, though. Callie picked up the quill to start working through it again when her phone rang. She fished it out of her pocket and saw Mike's name. Excited to fill him in, she answered quickly.

"Hey! I was just about to call you! You'll never believe what I just found out about Frank and Mae! Where are you? Are you headed home soon?" she asked.

"Callie?" His voice sounded distant. "Callie! Listen to me, you have to get—"

A loud cracking noise erupted on the other end of the line. Callie froze, her heart pounding as she called out for Mike. He didn't respond. Low, menacing laughter took Mike's place on the other end of the line. She demanded to know who it was, but it only made the stranger laugh more. Her hands started to tremble as she moved away from the desk.

"Who is this? What do you want? Where is my husband?" she hissed.

"Oh, he's right here, princess. He can't talk right now. He's a little tied up. You and I are going to have a nice long conversation, though, and maybe, just maybe, if you do everything I tell you, we'll let him go with just a few little bumps and bruises."

Callie swallowed. "What do you want? Money?"

He clicked his tongue. "Nothing so crass. We just want you three to take a little trip and not ever come back. All you need to do is get your brat, get in a taxi, and get the fuck out of the state. Once you've done that, we'll ship little Mike here wherever you want him."

"Please just let him go. If you want us to leave, we will; just give me back my husband."

"All in good time. It seems like we are on the same page. Now, I'm sure you know this goes without saying, but if you get smart with me or try to bring in some friends from that big city of yours, we're going to have problems. If you think I'm joking around, I'll pluck off a few of those typing fingers your husband loves so much and send them right on over—"

"No!" Callie screamed. "No, you don't need to do anything like that. I won't go to the police or anyone in the city, I promise you that. Please, just don't hurt him."

"Good, good. I thought you might say that. You've got twenty-four hours to leave town with your daughter. Take whatever you want. I really don't fucking care, but you're not ever coming back, so make it count. If I catch wind of you talking to the cops or anything like that, I'll start hacking off bits and pieces of your husband here. Hell, I might do it just to prove my point, got it, bitch? I'm in charge now."

"Fine, when will you let him go?" Callie asked.

"You'll have him back when I'm good and fucking ready! If you keep asking questions, you'll be getting him back in bits and pieces! Understood?" he snarled.

Callie sobbed. "Yes, I'm sorry. Okay, I'll do it."

A whistle blew in the background. It triggered a memory of their first trip into town. Callie's heart started to race.

"Good girl. Now, if you do everything just like we plan, you'll see your husband again before the week is up. No funny business, toots."

"Please, just let me talk to him—"

The line went dead before she could finish her sentence. Callie stared at the phone in her hand for a few seconds before snapping out of it. She knew she'd heard the train whistle before, but she couldn't remember where it was. There was an old depot the coal mines in surrounding counties still used on occasion. It didn't stop every day but maybe once or twice a week. She'd promised to leave and never come back, but her husband needed her. She grabbed the last of Benjamin's journals and darted for the door. There was only one man who could help her now.

39

Callie raced through the woods, stopping just long enough to see Lizzy and Gale enjoying their picnic at the other end of the lake. The pair waved to her. She waved back despite feeling like her world was coming down around her. If this plan didn't work, Lizzy might not have parents left. There was no question in her mind about what needed to be done, though. Mike would fight for her just as she was about to fight for him. She just didn't know the town, people, or layout nearly as well as he did. She was going to need Frank's help with all that. Armed with the information that these people may have killed his daughter and grandkids insured, he would help her. Not that it was ever questioned in her mind. In the short time they'd known each other, Callie had come to regard Frank as a friend and even some sort of family.

When she reached his cabin, she frantically pounded on the door. His shocked expression only intensified when he took in her disheveled appearance. He stepped aside to let her in without asking any questions as she started to tell him about the phone call and the train whistle she'd heard in the background. Once the flood-gates opened, Callie couldn't seem to stop talking. Before long, she found herself rambling about Benjamin's ghost and everything she'd learned from him in his journals. With two hot cups of coffee in hand, Frank sat down at the small oak table and patted her shoulder until she finally stopped to take a breath.

"They have him, Frank. They have Mike, and now they want me to leave with Lizzy, but I don't think I'll ever see him again if I do."

"What's this you were going on about Collin and the sheriff now? You lost me at that part."

"They're tied to this somehow. Collin wants the land. I don't know why she's helping him, but it's the only thing that makes sense. Mike was going to take everything and drop it off at the post office. I don't know if he even made it. The paperwork had the last page of the deed. Collin and the sheriff think he can sign it over, but it's not possi-ble. Even if he wanted to, it's just not able to be done; the original Grant investors made sure of that."

"What? I'm sorry, sweetheart, you lost me again."

"Oh," Callie muttered. "Right, I'm sorry. I'm so worried about Mike. Do you think we should call the police?"

"You said something about another part to the deed?" Frank reminded her.

"Yeah, we found it in his desk. He'd kept it tucked away. I guess he didn't trust anyone anymore at the end, but it basically says that even after the last Grant heir dies, the property can't be touched for like five years, and all money has to be donated. Only then can someone else take over."

"Five years?" Frank repeated. "Jesus."

Callie glared at him. "That's not really the problem here, Frank. They have Mike! If they find the other part to that deed, they will come after Lizzy and me next. I need to get Mike. Listen, I heard a train whistle, but I don't remember where that old station is at, do you?"

"Of course I do. I've been here my whole life. Boy, that sure is something. The Grants sure knew how to keep what was theirs. Bastards didn't want to share with anyone."

"Frank, I know what was used to kill the kids and Benjamin. If we can find that knife, it will have either Collin or the sheriff's fingerprints all over it. It's a cross... it was made of solid gold and engraved all over with different pictures. Have you seen anything like that?"

"Now, how did you go figuring out that?" he asked. "No offense, but that sounds like something out of a fiction book."

"It's not, I promise. I wish I could explain. I've been seeing things, ghosts and spirits. I think the sheriff killed Mae and Maria in the same fashion but sank their bodies in the lake. I promise once we get Mike back, we'll find them and lay them to rest...I know how much you cared for them."

Frank tapped his fingers on the table, never taking his eyes off her. "You got all that from some journals? The old fart was better at keeping records than I thought. Well, I reckon we should get on with things. I'll get some supplies rounded up, and we'll get you back to your husband."

Her eyes widened. "Really? Thank you, Frank, so much. I promise you always have a home here."

"I know. I've worked too hard and given up too much to see it all go to waste now."

Callie let out a sigh of relief as he grabbed a duffle bag and set it on the table. She watched him rummage around the small cabin for a few minutes, tossing in a large hatchet, rope, and tape before burying her face in her hands. It was all too much to take in at once. While he packed, though, there was still some good she could do.

"Did you and the sheriff ever have a thing?" she asked.

He snorted. "She don't play for my team, sweetheart. Old crow never liked Benjamin or me, though she took a shining to Mae. Always was trying to get her to skip out and start a new life. I think she loved her secretly. Course, Mae didn't swing that way, at least not to my knowledge."

Callie chuckled. "Well, I think you of all people would know what she liked."

Frank paused. "What's that supposed to mean now?"

She shrugged. Frank looked genuinely confused by what she'd said. He'd stopped packing altogether now and looked at her. Callie swallowed under his questioning gaze, her cheeks flushing.

"Well, you know, you and Mae had a thing," she finally admitted.

Frank burst into laughter. "Sweetheart, I think you've got your stories mixed up. Mae and I never had a thing. There was always a touch of tension between us but nothing more than two young kids and hormones. She only ever had eyes for old Benjamin."

Her jaw dropped. "She never got the chance to tell you, did she?"

Frank raised his eyebrow. "What?"

"Oh, Frank, you and Mae did have something; you just don't remember. There was a night not long before Maria was born when you got drunk and slept with a woman. You couldn't remember who—"

"How do you know about that?" Frank growled.

"Benjamin wrote it in his journal."

"I never told him about that night," he snarled.

"You didn't have to tell him. The woman you slept with did. That was Mae, Frank. She told Benjamin what had happened. Maria was your daughter."

Frank froze, a look of horror briefly racing across his features before he turned away from Callie. She wanted to go to him and give him some comfort, but she saw the tremble of rage in his shoulders. The poor man just realized how much he'd lost at the hands of Collin and his accomplice. She wanted to be patient with him, but every moment that passed was a moment closer to death for Mike. Before long, the sun would be setting and Gale would need to leave. With no one else to watch over Lizzy, Callie didn't know what she would do. They needed to make a move on Mike's captors and fast.

"I'm so sorry," she said quickly. "I thought you knew. Maria must not have gotten the chance to tell you before she died...I can't imagine what you're going through right now."

Frank ignored her words and set about gathering supplies again. She couldn't fathom what else they would need. He already seemed prepared for just about any scenario. The only thing missing was a gun. He turned to see her looking over the bag and chuckled.

"Cat got your tongue all of a sudden?" he asked.

She grinned. "No, I'm just not real sure on how you plan on defending us."

Frank reached down, pulling up his pant leg and grabbing something tucked into his boot.

"I never leave home without this," he whispered. "We've been through a lot together."

Frank laid the knife on the table in front of Callie. Her blood ran cold. It was the golden cross. All the pieces of the puzzle started to fall together. The sheriff had never been involved in the murders. She was nothing more than a convenient scapegoat. Callie wanted to scream but thought of Lizzy outside. She bit the inside of her lip to keep from crying out. She'd played right into Frank and Collin's hand. Now, all their fates were sealed.

Frank leaned down over her, his voice an ominous whisper. "Like I said, I've worked too hard and given up too much to see it all go to waste now."

40

*C*allie knew there was no point in trying to run. The tension in the air was enough to tell her that Frank knew the truth the same as she did. He had murdered everyone he claimed to care about in cold blood. Whether or not Colin had a hand in it was another question altogether. There was no doubt he was the mastermind behind the evil atrocities that had taken place. Yet Frank had been a willing if not even participant in the scheme.

For a fleeting moment, Callie had thought she'd seen remorse in Frank's eyes. The look was quickly covered by cold darkness she couldn't comprehend. The images of the brutal murders that Mike had shown her earlier in the week came flooding back. Her stomach rolled, she swallowed back the lump in her throat as she thought about the children. Perhaps there was still hope for Frank. It was apparent that he had killed Mae and Maria, but perhaps Colin was the truly evil spirit who had murdered two innocent children.

"Why?" Callie asked. "Why would you kill Mae and Maria?"

"That old hag had it coming," Frank growled. "She was filling old Benjamin's head with all sorts of fairy tales. She damn near had that old coot convinced that he should sell everything and run off to Mexico with her, like a pair of kids."

"So you were jealous?" Callie asked.

Frank snorted. "Not in the least. She was nothing but a local trollop. Anyone and everyone could have her if they wanted."

Callie shook her head. "You're wrong. Benjamin really cared for her and you both. You murdered a woman out of pure jealousy. You're just not man enough to admit it."

"Jealousy? Over what? She was a maid. And apparently not even a very good one at cleaning up her mess," he said with a chuckle. "Hell, I didn't even remember screwing the broad. I guess it makes sense then why her daughter was poking around. I must admit that little tidbit caught me by surprise."

Callie dropped her head, shaking it slowly. "You killed Maria because you thought she was getting close to solving her mother's murder? You're an idiot. She didn't care about that anymore. She wasn't snooping around for answers, at least not about that."

"What the hell are you talking about?" Frank barked.

"She was snooping around because you were her father!" Callie screamed. "She wanted to get to know you better! And what did she get for it? You murdered your own daughter in cold blood. Tell me, did you murder your grandchildren, too?"

"Do you have any idea what I've gone through on this property? How many little bitches like Mae, Maria, and you pass through? The number would shock you. There is no place for women here. Now, I tried to do the chivalrous thing and get you and your brat out of here, but you insisted on staying put. All of this is your fault, not mine."

"Chivalrous? You are a murderer! Where is my husband?" Callie seethed.

"Oh, we're going to get you two back together, don't you worry about that. I think it's about time for this whole charade to come to an end."

"You've lost your mind," she hissed.

Frank swung around to face her again. His eyes glistened with rage. A bolt of fear crept through her. All she could think about was her daughter playing joyfully on the other side of the lake. How long would it be before the pair tired of the later afternoon insects and returned to the house? Her stomach clenched in agony. She had to get to Mike, and they had to save Lizzy. Callie just needed to form a plan, but from the looks of things, she was running out of time. Frank whistled as he zipped up the bag, giving her a wink as she glared at him.

"I just want to know what kind of man could kill his own family," Callie pressed.

"They weren't my family. Only Benjamin mattered to me, and he was going to cut me off to be with that bitch. After all the years I put into this place, you'd think I'd deserve more. No, not old Benny boy. He said he'd leave me 'a little something' to get by but that Grants weren't the charitable type. Can you believe that? My entire life, I took care of his kind, my whole damn life."

"You'll never get the property. Benjamin made sure of that."

"Oh yeah? And who is going to know? That idiot Collin has the paperwork your husband was going to mail. Thanks for that, by the way. You two just kept telling me everything I needed to know to stay one step ahead. You were smart not to let your girl swim. How did you know about the bodies?"

The spirits. "I told you, Mae and Maria are still here, right along with the rest of them. Benjamin was never insane, was he?"

"Insane? No," Frank grinned. "Boy, you are a smart cookie, now aren't you? See, like I said, I've been here my whole life. While little Ben and his family were off at parties or one of their other houses, I was stuck here while my old man took care of the place. I got to know every little nook and cranny of that house."

Callie gasped. "You were the one Benjamin recorded on the camera!"

"The stupid son of a bitch never should have installed that," Frank growled. "I was so close to pushing him over the edge. Then he went and got some reasoning, and all talk of the place being haunted and spirits out to get him flew away. That was going to be my golden ticket. Drive him nuts and let him do the dirty work, but he loved those damn brats."

"Someone had to; they were murdered by their grand-father," Callie spat.

"They were nothing more than bastards, just like their mother. I did the world a service, probably saved them from a shit future of housework like their mom was enslaved to."

"So that's how you're justifying it? You think that makes everything okay? You won't get away with this."

"Little girl, I already have. Now, we've wasted enough time. We've got to get you and Mike back together for the big reunion. Do you want to yell for Lizzy to come over here, or should I?" Frank asked.

Callie's eyes widened.

He grinned. "Probably best if I do. We don't want anyone getting spooked after all, right?"

Frank grabbed the roll of duct tape sitting on the table. Her body froze in panic. She could still hear the girls across the lake. The smooth surface of the water always acted like a sound conductor. Sometimes at night, while sitting on the porch, they could hear the radio in Frank's cabin playing despite the long distance between the homes. There was a chance if she screamed, the girls might hear her. No. She needed to keep his attention away from her daughter.

"If you touch her, you won't know where the copy is!" Callie blurted out.

Frank paused. "What the hell are you rambling on about now?" he asked.

"The deed! The full one, at least. I made a copy of it and took it away from Grant Manor."

"You're bluffing," he snarled.

She shook her head. "No. It was right after discovering that Mike had omitted me from the home loan and the house deed. I was protecting myself."

His jaw twitched, a thick vein protruding between his eyes. "Where is it?"

Callie pursed her lips. "I'm not telling you anything until I've seen my husband, and Lizzy isn't going anywhere with us. I've got family up north. You send her there and get Mike back, then we will talk."

"Or maybe I'll just go out there, drown her and the sitter in the lake, then start torturing your husband till you talk. How would you like that now?" He was enraged.

Before she could react, he grabbed the duct tape off the table and smacked a piece over her mouth while one hand worked her wrists. Callie tried to scream and warn the girls, but Frank was twice her size and surprisingly fit despite his outward appearance. Once it was clear she wouldn't be able to free herself, he sat down next to her and ripped the tape off her mouth. Her lips cracked as little tears formed.

"Now, let's try this again. Where is the copy?"

Callie burst into tears. "I want to see my husband! Let me send Lizzy away at least, please."

Frank glared at her as he pulled out his phone. "We've got a problem," he hissed into it before walking away from her.

Her lips were no longer bound, but she didn't dare scream. The images of Vera and Marcus came back to her. She couldn't let her daughter end up with the same fate.

Frank spoke in hushed whispers for a few minutes while glaring at her from across the room. When he finished, a menacing smile had returned. He grabbed his knife from the table.

"See now, that's why I keep the little shit around. He's always coming up with a plan B."

Callie filled her lungs to scream, but Frank moved with decisive speed. For the second time that day, her world went dark.

Her head was pounding. Even the dim light above felt too intense for Callie to open her eyes all the way. Particles of dust assaulted her nose. It started to tingle instantly. She'd completely forgotten her allergy medication the last few days. There really was no need as long as she didn't go into the house's musky basement. A groan slipped past her lips as she struggled through the pain. Her wrists were still bound by tape, but now it was joined by a rope tied tightly around her ankles.

Something moved in the darkness next to her. She tensed instantly, pleading with her eyes to drop their blur and offer some help. A noise came from the figure. It wiggled around on the floor for a moment before going limp again. When her name came from the figure's lips, she nearly screamed with relief. It was Mike, lying on the ground. Slowly, her vision adjusted to the low light, and she was able to make out her husband's features for the most part. He was bound with the same rope used on her, though his wrists were contorted behind his back. Callie's sat in her lap.

"Jesus, Mike, are you okay?" she whispered.

He groaned.

"Please wake up, sweetheart. Mike!" Callie hissed. "Dammit, they are going to kill our daughter!"

Her words seemed to rouse something in her husband. As he slowly started to sit up, Callie saw the full extent of his injuries and gasped. His left eye was swollen completely shut, a purple hue telling her it would look like that for several weeks to follow. A thick trail of dried blood ran down his neck behind his right ear. When he moved, he favored his right shoulder. She couldn't fathom the abuse he'd endured at Collin's twisted hands. There was no time for her to worry about what she couldn't change, though. If their family was going to survive the next hour, they needed to have their wits about them.

"Dammit, man," she growled.

He blinked, shaking off the haze. "I'm here. What the hell? Where are we?"

"We're in the basement of the manor. Keep your voice down. They are right upstairs, and I don't know where Lizzy is. The last time I was awake, she was still playing with Gale at the lake. Oh God, Mike. What are we going to do?"

"She's okay," Mike whispered, his throat dry. "That little shit drugged me right before we left that warehouse, but I started to come round when I heard Frank's voice. Sorry, sweetheart, it's all so fucking groggy still. They had a bag over my head and must have tossed me down the steps because I blacked out again after that. Frank said they were out at the lake still. He fed Gale some lie about fumigating the house and to steer clear."

"Well, at least she's okay for now. I know what he's waiting for," Callie said.

She quickly filled him in on everything that had happened since they'd last spoken. His cheeks flushed red with rage as he listened to Callie unfold the story of murder and deception that Frank had lived. It was easy to feel the same way he did.

"Collin is no better," Mike growled. "He and Benjamin had a huge falling out right after he tried to sue him for the property. It was right after Maria started asking around about Frank and her mom, which makes sense now. Collin was under the impression that she had found out he had killed her mother, just like Frank. Collin enjoyed talking about himself. He thinks he's God's gift to this community. One night, he was at the manor, snooping around when lo and behold, he stumbled on Frank mid-murder with Maria."

"Oh my God," Callie whispered.

"Yeah, he's a real piece of work. It sounds like they were made for each other. Anyway, they both realized that night that they wanted the same thing and formed a twisted little bond. So they think that you have another copy of the real deed somewhere?"

Callie nodded.

"Well, that was smart thinking on your part. I don't want to think about what would have happened if they'd brought you to the warehouse. Lizzy probably wouldn't have made it this far. You've done great, babe."

"Yeah, but we are running out of time. When they come down here, they're going to want to know where it's at."

"What about a bank? Somewhere in a vault far away."

"What am I going to do when they take me there and the teller looks at me like I've lost my mind?"

"I don't know," Mike admitted. "I'm just trying to buy us some more time...wait! It's after five now! The bank is closed, and it will be all weekend!"

"Do you really think they're going to wait around that long to get what they want?" she asked.

"Jesus, I have no idea what to expect anymore. You're right, though; they'll never wait. They'll kill all three of us wait out the hold on the deed."

Callie sighed. She felt beyond defeated, as if she were already a walking corpse. Every part of her body ached. Despite trying to force her mind to find any path to safety, she was struggling just to stay conscious. Her stomach continued to do somersaults. She couldn't remember the last time she'd felt so sick, if ever. A lump was already starting to form in her throat as the dust particles assaulted her already weary senses.

"Jesus, Callie. What did I get us into? I'm so sorry. This is all my fault. I can't believe we let that monster play with our little girl. My God."

"Don't blame yourself. We thought this place was our dream home. It wasn't just you. Frank had us both fooled, and Collin knew we needed that money. Anyone in our position would have done the same."

"I just can't stop thinking about all the times we've let her wander down to the lake with him. God, with those bodies…."

"Don't think about it, Mike," Callie advised. "Just don't let it get to you right now."

"I'm so sorry," he repeated. "My grandfather was right. This house brings nothing but pain and suffering to Grants."

"Don't start talking like that. The suffering was all thanks to Frank and Collin. It wasn't some silly curse, it wasn't evil spirits, it was two shitty killers who deserve everything they have coming to them. We will find a way out of this. Do you hear me?"

Mike nodded. "I don't know what I'd do without you, woman."

"Jesus, I want to scream," she stammered.

"I know. We can't do that, though. Gale is going to be leaving soon, and she'll bring Lizzy back to the house. We have to get out of here. Can you get the tape off your wrists?"

Callie shook her head. "Even if I could, I can see the end of a zip tie under it. He must have wrapped me back up after knocking me out."

"All right, if I lift my legs up to your hands, do you think you can try to untie the rope on my feet?"

"I might be able to. All we can do is try," Callie replied.

Mike scooted across the floor. Every noise sounded amplified in the empty space. Callie cringed as the folding chair creaked beneath the added weight of her husband's legs. She tugged at the rope. Her fingers felt stiff. They lacked the blood flow needed for her to grip the knot. The situation was getting desperate, though. Dropping her head, she took the knot between her teeth and tugged at it. Upstairs, they could hear the men moving toward the steps. They were almost out of time.

"Stop!" Mike hissed.

She dropped it instantly, and he scooted away from her, his legs folded to the side, right next to his bound hands. The position looked incredibly painful, but his fingers worked furiously to loosen the bonds. The basement door opened, flooding the steps with light and fresh air for a split second before slamming shut again. The matching sound of heavy footsteps sent a chill through Callie's spine. They still didn't have a plan together. Her eyes darted one last time to Mike. His fingers were cramping and the knot was still tight.

Collin looked exactly as she'd expected. A spiteful entitlement filled his hollow eyes. She wanted to leap from the chair and knock him out. At least she'd get in a good shot before one or both of them beat her into oblivion. There was no reasoning with men like them. Callie knew the only possibility her family had of escape was by taking out the two men before they had the chance to hurt them first. Otherwise, they would keep hunting the couple. Their corrupt community would protect them just as they had Frank with the murders before.

42

"Well, well, well," Frank said. "It looks like our lovebirds are finally awake. I was just about to toss you into the lake to see if you were still alive."

"Should I grab a bag of cement?" Collin asked with a grin. "I saw some trash bags upstairs, and I know you've got some tape. We can do it just like the last one; poke a few holes in them…."

"Let's not get ahead of ourselves. After all, we wouldn't want her to go showing anyone the deed."

Collin laughed. "Oh right, I forgot she was still pretending to have that. What do you think? Should we let her know?"

"Awe, I was going to let them squirm a little bit first!" Frank moaned. "Dammit, boy. I've worked on this longer than you have."

Callie realized, at that moment, they knew the truth. Of course, they'd figured it out, but how? She had to stall for more time. It was such a shock to see the stark difference in Frank, though. She felt like she was looking at two different people when she compared the Frank from before. He'd played the part so well. Everything from helping Callie and Mike to treating Lizzy like his own granddaughter had her shaken. It wasn't right. Nothing about what was happening was right or fair.

"What makes you think I'm bluffing?" she snapped with renewed anger. "I can't wait for both of you to get exactly what you've got coming. You'll never get away with this."

"You stupid bitch," Collin hissed. "There is only one bank in this county, and I own all three locations. We've had eyes on you since day one. That's right, we've been watching you. You might have thrown old Frank for a loop, but I know you never made a second copy. I've got cameras across from the only library in town where you can make copies."

Callie swallowed. "Please, let our daughter go. She has nothing to do with this."

"She's got everything to do with this," Frank growled. "She's just another little spoiled Grant brat, ready to take whatever she wants without working in life. She might look cute now, but in a few years, she'll be a bloodsucker, just like the rest of you. Don't worry, we've got a special plan for her."

Mike yelled. "I'll kill you—"

Collin's hand collided with his cheek in an instant, sending Mike toppling back down onto his side. His head smacked the cement with sickening force. Callie started to tremble as she called out to her husband, pleading with him to wake up again. She didn't want to be left there alone with the men. Mike had to wake up. Her pleas didn't seem to faze the two kidnappers. They drowned out her cries as they continued to formulate their next move.

"You said it yourself. Those other two would be back soon. We have to get this place set up perfect for the story to work. What do we know about the girl with their kid?"

Frank shrugged. "Not much, don't really care. It will just be one more tragedy of Grant Manor."

Callie burst into laughter. Both men paused their conversation and looked at her skeptically. She didn't stop until Frank stepped forward and raised his hand to hit her. She shrank away, falling silent instantly, but the smile on her lips persisted. Callie had one last chance to save them all, or at least the younger two.

"Oh my God," she faked shock. "You really don't know, do you? Oh, Frank, I expected this from you but not you, Collin. You really didn't do your research? Gale isn't just some random kid I brought in off the street. She's going to be missed. People are going to ask a lot of questions, I promise you that. Plus, Mike made a big fuss at the station and called his buddies in New York last night. If you were smart, you'd get rid of her and not with murder, you pigs. At least if my family has to die and you're dumb enough to kill her, too, then I know you'll get caught."

"Frank, she's lying again," Collin reasoned. "You've said it yourself to me a dozen times. There is no trusting a woman. She's conniving just like the rest of them. Let's

MARIE WILKENS

just get a move on already. I want to start deciding where to put the new condominiums when this place is burned to the ground."

Callie scoffed. "You'll be in jail before the pile stops smoking, dumbass. There is just one thing I want to know. Which one of you cocksuckers was the one to kill the kids?"

The men exchanged looks, but it was the flush in Collin's cheeks that gave him away. Frank continued to glare at Callie, but her smile never wavered. She shrugged as if she didn't have a care in the world. In reality, she didn't. She'd reached a point of accepting her fate and Mike's at the very least. Now she was simply trying to bargain her way up to letting both girls go—Gale and her precious daughter.

"Go check it out," Frank barked. "You understand that internet search. Make sure she's not connected before we do this but make it fast. I'm tired of the games."

Collin grumbled under his breath but followed Frank's orders as he stormed back up the steps. The light flickered as the door slammed behind him. Frank's eyes darted to the swaying bulb. For a second, Callie was sure she saw fear in the old man's eyes. It was understandable, considering the extent of hatred he had among the spirits that still called Grant Manor their home. They'd been left to wander aimlessly, lost in a world belonging neither to the living nor the dead while Frank walked free. Rage filled Callie, the likes of which she'd only ever felt in the presence of Benjamin's spirit. She smiled at Frank menacingly.

"Little nervous there, Frank?" she asked. "You should

be. See, you were onto something when you said this house was evil. Although, I wouldn't call it 'evil' per se, more…possessed."

"Shut up," he growled. "I don't believe in that bullshit. Benjamin might have been that dumb but not me. It was easy to drive him insane when he was already so close. Everyone knew it, too."

The light at the top of the steps flickered again. This time it was joined by the bulb dangling above Frank's head. He jumped away from it as if it had stung him. Callie was starting to get under his skin. It was exactly what she wanted. The more anger she felt, it seemed the stronger Benjamin's spirit became. She'd made the discovery when the children only appeared to her when she was content. Different emotions gave strength to different entities depending on where they had left their souls in the mortal world. The innocent children were overall happy but not old Ben. Callie used the knowledge to her advantage.

"Benjamin is here, Frank, and he's not happy with what you did to him or the twins. I'm sure they'll be joining us soon, too," she sang quietly.

"I said shut up!" he yelled.

"Why, Frank? You've seen them, too, haven't you? That's why you got so scared on the porch. Mae and Maria are here, too, Frank. They'll be wanting a few words before you join them."

Frank stormed to where she was sitting. His hand moved with practiced speed, striking her mouth and instantly sending a shot of agony through her jaw. It amplified the pain in her head, but she refused to let herself cry out. The metallic taste of blood moved slowly across her tongue. Callie pinched her eyes closed, taking all the rage she felt over the injustice and channeling it into the room. The image shimmered when she opened her eyes again, but its figure was clear.

Benjamin Grant had come for his revenge.

Callie laughed. "Now you've done it, Frank. I tried to help you, but I don't think Benjamin is the forgiving type, not at all."

The lights flickered, immersing the room in darkness. A blood-curdling scream filled the room before being snuffed out by an eerie silence.

43

*E*ach time the bulb flickered, another horrifying scene was captured in Callie's mind. Above her, she could hear Frank's accomplice yelling for him to open the door. Her eyes darted to the top of the steps as the bulb flashed. She saw the ghost children huddled together, both holding the knob with all their might as they looked away from the scene unfolding on the basement floor. Callie couldn't blame them. Had she been free, she would be shielding the spirit's from the horrors as well. Benjamin was angry.

Though Frank had claimed not to see the spirits before, Callie was positive he could see the one standing over him. In the darkness, Benjamin had gotten Frank onto the ground. A trail of blood ran along the cement floor behind Frank. The source of the blood became evident with another blip of light. Callie saw the blade sticking out of the man's thigh. She had little doubt Benjamin had placed it there for him. Next to her, Mike stirred and bolted upright as he took in the scene in front of him.

He moved with lightning speed that Callie doubted she possessed in that terrifying moment. Without a second thought as to what was happening, Mike frantically worked on untying his ankles. It was a slow process despite his best attempts. The ropes were bound in hard coils. Callie's attention was split between the scene in front of her and helping her husband get free. She dove off the chair onto the floor next to Mike. The rush of adrenaline had given her fingers the boost they needed to work through the lack of circulation.

"Jesus," Mike hissed. "Am I hallucinating?"

Callie shook her head vigorously. "No. Don't look at it. Let's just get you free and get out of here."

"Look."

She didn't want to turn but couldn't stop herself. Morbid curiosity had set in. It was something you'd expect to see in a movie but never in your own home. Callie's heart lurched despite herself at the look of pure fear in Frank's eyes. There was no justice in what was happening to him. Benjamin reached down and, with concentrated effort, pulled the blade from Frank's leg. He screamed out in pain again, kicking frantically at the spirit, though his foot went right through him. Benjamin laughed.

"You never thought I'd come back for you, did you now, Frankie?" the spirit mused. "You've been a very bad man. Do you know what happens when you can't move on? You're stuck in the middle, forever repeating your own death."

"I'm sorry," Frank stammered. "Please, Ben, old friend, it wasn't like that. Mae was trying to play you for a fool. I was just protecting you! You know I didn't kill those twins of yours now. I'd never do something like that."

"You greedy little prick," Benjamin growled. "I should have listened to Mae when she told me the kind of man you were. She knew what you kept hidden from me, a monster. Well, there is a place for men like you."

"I never did anything to you or yours," Frank stammered indignantly.

"No? Where are my Mae and Maria now then?"

"I don't—"

"I can tell you where they are, Frankie boy. They are right here with me," Benjamin whispered.

"Those bitches are lying!" Frank screamed.

The blade moved with inhuman speed, plunging into Frank's other thigh. He screamed so loud Callie knew that Gale and Lizzy had to hear it. She tore her attention away. Mike sensed the renewed fear in her and quickly aided in his own rescue. Finally, they had his hands and feet free. He ripped the tape from Callie's hands, grabbing the zip tie and pulling it apart despite the blood that appeared between his fingers. As it cut into his flesh, Callie sobbed softly. They were so close to being free. The tie gave way. With no time for celebration, Mike grabbed her hand and darted for the cellar door leading to the outside.

Before they could unlock the hatch, a figure materialized in front of them, blocking the path. Callie gasped.

She'd only ever seen Maria up close, but Mae was a different story. Her death had gone unavenged for many years. The flesh now barely clung to her mostly decayed body. Bones protruded from her hands, held together only by tendons as she raised a finger and started to wag it at them. The ghost shook her head, droplets of water falling to the ground with bits of pond scum and hair.

"I'm not taking orders from a fucking ghost," Mike snapped.

He dropped Callie's hand and tried to walk through Mae. She laughed and shoved him backward. Mike stumbled and fell on his rear, unscathed. The look of shock on his face was matched by Callie as she turned back to the spirit. Mae wasn't nearly as transparent as Benjamin nor the children, yet Callie had seen Maria, who looked as solid as Mae did now. She stepped away from Mae. For whatever reason, the woman didn't want them to leave yet, and it didn't look like they were going to be given much of a choice in the matter.

"Mike, I think the longer a spirit is trapped here, the more power they have. She's stronger than the others."

"I don't care. I want to get my daughter and burn this place to the ground. They can have the two men. Let them get what they have coming."

"I think we should trust her."

"Help me!" Frank screamed. "For fuck's sake! Help me!"

The couple turned to see Frank now pressed against the farthest wall of the basement. Benjamin's spirit was still towering over him, though he was starting to flicker and fade. Mike saw the look of guilt in Callie's eyes and jumped to his feet, grabbing her before she could go to him. An instant later, as Callie struggled against Mike, she saw a figure appear at Benjamin's side. It was Mae. The blade slipped from his grip and into hers. She kneeled over Frank, whispering something to him as the blade lifted higher above his chest.

In the flash of an eye, the blade dropped. Callie buried her head in Mike's chest as she squeezed her eyes shut. The sound was enough as the metal punctured his chest with unnatural force. The scream that had filled the basement turned into a gurgling before finally, there was no sound left at all. Still, Callie clutched Mike, afraid to believe it was really all over. Everything around them was shrouded in darkness as the lights flickered off. The seconds seemed to drag on for an eternity as the couple clung to each other in the darkness. Even the pounding at the top of the steps was gone. The lights slowly started to hum back to life. Callie took a ragged breath and opened her eyes.

For a moment, she thought she was dreaming. The basement stood empty except for her and Mike. Had it not been for the chair and various items the men had used to restrain them, no one would be able to tell what had transpired only seconds before. There was no sign of the spirits, which she'd expected. By some force she couldn't comprehend, Frank was gone as well. There was no trace of him or the blade in sight. Briefly, Callie had wondered if he'd recovered and taken off up the steps somehow, but there wasn't a single drop of blood anywhere. There was no time to process what they were seeing.

"He's gone," Mike whispered. "Hurry, we need to find Lizzy and Gale."

"We'll cover more ground if we split up. There is no way they didn't hear that."

"You go out the cellar door. I'll go through the house to see if I can't get the drop on Collin. Get the girls and get out of here."

"I'm not leaving you alone here," Callie said.

Mike grabbed her shoulders, pulling her into his arms as he kissed her passionately. "Callie, please promise me that you will get Lizzy away from this place. Plus, I'm not alone. I don't think this house is done just yet. It wasn't Frank who killed the twins. Benjamin isn't going to let Collin get away from him."

"Please be careful," she pleaded.

He grinned. "Don't worry, us Grants are a tough lot. I'll see you and Lizzy soon, I promise."

Callie nodded, though she wasn't sure she believed him. She watched Mike head for the steps before turning and peeking out the cellar door. The sun was barely starting to dip in the sky. Silently, she said a prayer not only for herself but for her husband as well.

44

From what Callie could see, the coast was clear. She crept out of the basement, her gaze instantly moving along the lake's horizon as she searched for Gale and Lizzy. In the distance, she could make out the shape of their blanket and basket. They must have come running at the first sign of commotion inside. Her heart lurched. Without knowing how much time had passed, they could be anywhere.

Callie crept around the side of the house as she kept her eyes trained for any sign of movement. Her slow pace felt excruciating but necessary as the trimmed grass crunched beneath her feet. Poking her head around the corner first, she let out a sigh of relief to find Gale and Lizzy on the porch. They were facing the door and away from her. She moved a little farther, wanting to run to her daughter and wrap the child in the safety of her arms. As she moved to get a better view, her blood went cold.

Collin was standing in the doorway, a small pistol

pointed in the girls' direction. Standing between them and the killer was Mike. He had one hand up in surrender while the other was wrapped behind his back, protectively holding Lizzy behind him. The spirits who had been too helpful before were nowhere to be seen. Perhaps they'd used what abilities they had to rid the family of Frank. Callie was grateful for their help, but it still left Collin. He had the crazed look of a cornered animal; his voice trembled when he spoke.

"Tell me what you did to Frank," he demanded.

"Take it easy now, pal. There is still time for you to leave here right now," Mike promised. "You can head for the border, and we can lay all this on Frank."

"No. No! You tell me where he is. Did you make a deal with him, too, huh? Is this a setup? Where is he?"

"Come on, you heard what happened down there," Mike muttered. "Let the girls get some space from us, and we can talk. Lizzy...she's too young to hear—"

"Daddy," Lizzy interrupted. "You don't have to send me away."

Callie's heart sank. The brave little girl had no idea how much danger they were in. Mike just wanted them at a safe distance. At close range, there was no way to tell if his body alone would be enough to protect Lizzy if Collin decided to fire it off. The more he spoke, the more she picked up on the signs of panic. She'd endured a fair amount of crisis training at her work in a city like New York. Hostage situations in hospitals were all too common.

"Yeah, 'Daddy,'" Collin mocked. "Why send her away?

Don't you want her to know what you did to her old pal, Frank?"

"You stop it!" Lizzy yelled. "Daddy didn't do anything to him, and he was a bad man! Marcus told me so. He wanted to hurt my mommy and daddy, and they stopped him!"

"Who stopped him?" Collin demanded. "Huh? Shut up your kid, or I'll put a bullet in her."

"My grandpa and his friends stopped him," Lizzy mumbled.

Collin clicked the safety off the gun.

"Lizzy, be quiet right now," Mike hissed. "Let them go, Collin. You and I can sort this out. We can load up in my truck and drive away."

Collin's eyes lit up. "I've got a better idea." His tone rose. "Why don't you come out of hiding there, Mrs. Grant, and you and I can go for a little drive."

"Over my dead body," Mike hissed.

The gun dropped down to Mike's stomach as Collin pulled back the hammer. "Did you know the torso is the best place to shoot someone if you want it to go through?"

"Stop!" Callie screamed.

She emerged from the side of the house with her hands raised. She wasn't going to let anyone get shot. Things had already escalated beyond reason. If he wanted to take her, fine. She would find a way to escape, but even if she couldn't, it would get the monster away from Lizzy. That was all that mattered.

She still had her father, and Mike was a good parent. Her hands shook as she stopped just short of the porch steps. Lizzy called out and tried to run to her as soon as she saw her mother. Thankfully, Mike held the little girl back, his eyes locked on Callie's. Her heart was pounding. She loved them both so much it was almost unbearable.

Collin's victorious grin caught her attention as he moved down the steps, keeping the gun leveled on Lizzy the entire way. He grabbed ahold of Callie by the back of her neck, dragging her toward Mike's pickup. He shoved her into the driver's seat before climbing in next to her. She tried not to sob as she buckled her seatbelt, desperately trying to stall him.

Despite her best attempts to explain to him that she couldn't drive a standard well at all, Collin insisted on her taking the wheel. At every command, she followed until they were moving slowly down the driveway. Callie watched Mike's pained expressions each time the clutch ground in his beloved antique.

"Listen, you don't need me anymore, okay? Just let me slip out here. You're not going to make it far with me behind the wheel. I don't know what I'm doing."

"Well, you better figure it out really quick, bitch. If you think I won't turn around and sink a bullet into that pretty little girl of yours, you've got another thing coming. I know you two killed Frank."

"Don't you see? None of that matters anymore. It's over," she exclaimed.

"Not so fast. You are my meal ticket out of here. We're going to go to the bank, you and I. Then after that, we'll make our way down to Mexico, just like your old man said to do."

"And then what? Do you really think they are just going to let a child killer go?"

"You better pray they do because if I catch wind of the law coming after me, I'll be right back here to snipe your precious little princess."

Callie swallowed the growing lump in her throat. If Collin got away, she would never get another restful night of sleep again. Lizzy would never be safe, and justice would never be done for Vera and Marcus. The thought of the two children conjured their images. Collin was rattling on about his plans for Mexico, oblivious to the presence of the two spirits. A wave of calm washed over Callie. Vera spoke. It became clear that Collin, a non-believer, couldn't see them at all.

"Thank you for helping us," Vera said.

Callie smiled at her and nodded. She didn't want to speak and risk drawing Collin's attention.

"Mommy gave you something. It's in your pocket. Don't look now, though. You aren't going to want to miss this next part. It should be fun. You should probably hold on to something."

"What?" Callie stammered as the trance broke.

Suddenly, the steering wheel jerked to the left without her command. She didn't even have time to react as the pickup plunged headfirst down the sloping side of the property. Collin screamed and reached for the wheel, struggling against the unseen force that was now in control. Callie pressed the brake, but there was no response from the truck. The children appeared again,

Marcus jumping up from the seat and into Callie's flailing arms.

Her maternal instinct took control, and she wrapped her arms around him, closing her eyes and holding him tight as the truck plowed into the line of trees.

* * *

SHE WOKE in their bedroom with a start. Instantly, she started to search her body for injuries from the crash, but nothing felt or looked out of place. As a matter of fact, she felt well-rested and perfectly content. Callie didn't have time to process anything before the bedroom door opened and a woman in her late fifties came in. She smiled at Callie before sitting on the edge of the bed. It was strange how familiar the woman seemed.

"I tried to get Ben to come to say his farewells, but he's a stubborn old fool and ready to go. You know how persistent men can get when they're done with the task at hand."

Callie gasped. "You're Mae! I'm sorry, I didn't recognize you."

"With flesh?" she offered with a playful smile. "I would think not! Though, I much prefer this version."

"Oh God," she whispered. "Am I...am I dead?"

"Heavens, no! Do you think I'd let those two rotten grandkids of mine go through with a plan like that if you were going to be killed?" Mae scoffed. "I may be...or was a vengeful spirit, but you were always safe with us."

Callie looked around. "Then what is this?"

She shrugged. "We can call it a dream. You bumped your head, but you'll wake up. Crush a few aspirins in some whiskey, and you'll be right as rain tomorrow."

Mae smiled and looked out the bedroom window. "Now, you go and live your life. You've got a family of four to take care of."

"Oh, we only have one child…the other girl is just her sitter."

Mae's eyes moved away from the window where Callie could hear Maria and the children calling for her. They dropped down to Callie's abdomen, where her hands had instinctively come to rest. Suddenly, the nausea and fatigue all made sense.

The woman chuckled as she rose. "He's going to have a good heart, just like his mother."

45

"Callie!" Mike called.

She groaned as the world around her came into focus. Mike was kneeling on the grass next to her, tears streaming down his cheeks. Instantly, the smell of burning flesh pierced her nose. She sat up and saw the truck engulfed in flames about a hundred yards from where they were sitting in the grass. She hugged her husband tight as her eyes landed on the burnt corpse of her kidnapper lying on the ground.

"Lizzy!" she stammered.

"It's fine. As soon as I saw the truck veer off, I followed after. Gale took her inside and was calling the police when I left."

"Great, the sheriff is going to love this," Callie muttered. "How are we going to explain everything to her? She's never going to believe what really happened."

"I don't know. I'm just happy it's over," Mike admitted.

Mike held her for a few more minutes in stunned

silence before the sound of an approaching cruiser roused them. Callie gave Mike a confused look when she realized it wasn't the chief from their small town. Instead, a fit man in his late forties emerged. The pair met him at his car. Lizzy was in her mother's arms in an instant, and to their shock, Gale flew into the officer's arms as well. Suddenly, Callie was able to see the resemblance between them.

"I told you getting a summer job was bad for your health," he said to Gale before turning to the others. "Folks, I'm deputy Ryan Masters. We've got two more units, a fire truck, and an ambulance on the way. Now, my little girl here said this fella held you at gunpoint and tried to kidnap you?"

Callie's jaw dropped as she nodded.

"I must say, ma'am, that was some right quick-thinking running your truck into those trees."

"I-I told him I didn't know how to drive a standard," Callie stammered.

"So, who wants to start?" he asked.

Callie remembered what the children had said in the truck before it hit the trees. She felt the folded parchment in her pocket and reached inside. Tugging it out, she unfolded it. The letterhead was that of Frank. It was dated the week prior. She'd seen his penmanship before on different notes and lists for the house. It was unquestionably his handwriting, though Callie knew he'd never written it. She handed it over to the police officer. He raised an eyebrow and cleared his throat before reading it out loud.

"My name is Frank Langdon. I worked for Benjamin Grant until I murdered him…." Deputy Masters trailed off. "Whoa. Isn't that the crazy old rich guy who lived out here?"

Mike nodded. "Yeah, he was my grandfather. We just inherited the property and started digging into his death. You wouldn't believe the ride we've had."

"Let him finish," Callie hissed.

Masters continued reading. "In addition to killing him. I also killed his previous housekeepers, Mae and Maria Solis. You can find their bodies in the lake and the murder weapon in my home." He paused. "Folks, do you know where this man is at?"

Mike and Callie looked at each other before shaking their heads.

"No, we just found the note," Callie admitted.

Clearing his throat, he read on. "I'll never forgive myself for what I did. I drove Ben mad by using hidden halls in the manor and stabbing him from behind like a coward. None of the three deserved to die. Collin is the one who killed Vera and Marcus. He found out about the woman and insisted it was the only way to ever get our hands on the Grant money and property. I went along with it. I was happy to be a killer just like him. By the time you find this, I'll be in the Atlantic ocean, wearing the same cement shoes I made for Mae and Maria."

The officer folded the note back up. The group stood there in silence for a moment, each of them too shocked to speak. Callie fought the urge to let out a sigh of relief when he was done reading. It tied up just about every-thing perfectly.

"So this fella left this note, then probably let that Collin fella know he'd confessed."

"Right," Callie agreed. "That's why he came here. Collin wanted the note and to use me as a bargaining chip in case he got caught trying to flee to Mexico. I don't think he realized that Gale and Lizzy were here. He had us tied up in the basement but heard them outside. That was when Mike was able to get free and got me free. Honestly, I think we are all just happy this is over. We had no idea our groundskeeper could do such horrible things. How is it you're able to be here and not the local officers?"

Callie couldn't believe how easily she'd come up with the story. She'd barely had time to process what was happening since waking back up, but slowly, the memo-ries were being pieced together. It wasn't the truth, but it was the version they needed to learn and stick with unless they all wanted the local superstition of the Grants being insane to follow after them. Still, had it not been for the help of the spirits, there would have been an insurmount-able level of details they'd have to come up with reasons for.

He grinned. "Funny thing about the manor, it sits right on the county line. The Grants have always had the option to switch counties given how big the property is, but I don't think anyone ever made much effort to tell the old man about it. As far as I could tell, they all seemed to like the money the lake brought in each year."

Mike burst into laughter. "Well now, doesn't that just

make perfect sense? You know what? I think we are going to have to see about changing that. I can't think of a single reason why we would want to stay in this town."

A flurry of dust arose from the base of the driveway as the calvary pulled into the driveway. The firetruck made a beeline for the engulfed pickup and had the flames out before long as officers descended on Callie, Mike, and the others. Despite assuring them that they were uninjured, an EMT looked everyone over. Neither of them hesitated when the police asked to search the house and Frank's cabin. The couple followed the officers around for a few hours as the truck was hauled away pending their investigation. It was all routine. When the last of them left, Gale and her father, Mike, and Callie stood on the porch to wave them off. Mike kissed Callie's forehead, his hand slipping down her waist into her palm.

"Are you going to come inside, Mrs. Grant?" Mike asked.

She nodded and leaned into him as they listened to Lizzy sing along with the radio inside. Everything about the moment was perfect. She still couldn't believe everything they'd endured in the last few weeks. Yet somehow, it all felt like the distant past in just the span of a few hours. Never before had Callie felt such a serene sense of peace at Grant Manor.

"Have you noticed how different it feels out here now?" Callie asked.

Mike nodded. "Yeah, it's a little weird. I didn't realize how much tension the house really had until it was gone. I can't believe all that was real. Do you think we will ever see the ghosts again, or...do you think they like...moved on?"

Callie chuckled. "I think they've all moved on, and it's long overdue."

She gasped. It had completely slipped her mind.

"Speaking of overdue," she hinted. "How would you feeling about adding one more to our trio?"

Mike's eyes lit up. "Yeah?"

She nodded, cradling her stomach.

His jaw dropped. "Wait, you mean you already are? Really?"

"Really," she whispered.

Mike let out a loud cheer, scooping his wife into his arms and spinning her around as they both laughed. They'd finally broken the curse of Grant Manor.

EPILOGUE

"*Y*ou know, I think the question America wants to know the answer to is this; how did you get inspired to write such a gripping novel?" she asked.

Mike blushed and grinned. "Honestly, Miranda, it was all my wife."

The audience erupted in a round of applause. Mike smiled at them and gave them a wave. It had been a wild six months since they'd first invested in Grant Manor, but now, the haunting story had brought some light to their lives. With Mike's book topping the charts and a mile-long waitlist to stay at the bed and breakfast, he couldn't think of a happier time in their lives.

"Well, that's touching. I hear you are expecting baby number two? Congratulations."

There was a second round of applause. Mike felt pride wash over him. Lizzy was as excited as her parents to be welcoming a new little bundle of joy into their growing family. She'd gone as far as offering to share her room with him, a notion both parents appreciated since the other rooms were booked full. Although it wasn't lost on him that the previous occupants had been siblings as well. He pushed the thought aside.

"Yes, a little boy, he's due in about three months now. We are beyond excited, and Callie, my wife, just rocks pregnancy so much. I can't believe how amazing she is."

"That's wonderful. Now that you've had a taste of a bestseller, can we expect a second novel anytime soon?"

It had taken him two months to write the book and only three weeks for his publisher to approve the haunting tale and put a rush on the publication. Thinking back, it still shook him to know that the story the world had fallen in love with wasn't a mere work of fiction. He'd lived through every harrowing ordeal but had carefully crafted the details as a work of pure fiction.

Of course, no one would ever believe the account was anything other than just that. The official records had been released and bodies pulled from their resting places. In the end, everything matched up with what Callie and Mike had told the authorities. Some people had despised the couple for bringing the tale to light. Fortunately for them, they were no longer part of the same hateful community.

He laughed and shook his head. "Honestly, I think I nailed it with the first one. The entire process is one I'm not sure I want to do again, but who knows what the future holds, right?"

"Well said, plus, with the sales already, you could probably retire!" she said with a laugh. "We are just about wrapped up here, but is there anyone you want to say hello to?"

Mike nodded and looked at the camera. "Hi, Lizzy! Hi, Callie! I can't wait to get back home and see you both!"

"There you have it, ladies and gentlemen. America's hot new author and hopping business owner, Michael Grant!"

He was happy when, an hour later, he was flying back home. The jet was owned by his publisher, but as the next big author, they were happy to let him use it. Mike rested his head on the seat before closing his eyes and thinking about his wife and daughter. The little boy on the way was already named after his legacy.

Like it or not, Benjamin Grant had saved all of their lives that night in the basement. He deserved some recognition. His mind raced back to the interview. It was the last one until after the baby was born. No, Mike had no desire to write a second book at all. He'd always dreamed of being a famous author, but the more time he'd spent at the manor with his wife and daughter, the more he'd come to realize that was his home, and it would be forever.

With the manor now operating as a successful bed and breakfast, they'd taken Frank's old cabin and converted it into a writing lodge for Mike. It was the perfect little retreat for him when the house reminded him of what they'd endured. A chill moved through the airplane's cabin as he tugged a blanket over his legs. Someday soon, he planned on returning to the manor and never leaving again. The old place was starting to grow on him. It almost had a mind of its own.

* * *

"Boy, he sure does look good on the big screen," Gale joked.

Callie laughed. "Don't I know it! How do you think I landed in this position? It's that damn smile of his! I'm going to miss you so much when you go back to school. Are you sure you don't want to stay here with us forever?"

Gale laughed, folding the last of Lizzy's clothes for Callie despite her protests. The afternoon had zapped all of her energy. Between the new bookings, hiring staff, and trying to replace Gale, she'd barely stopped running all day. When her phone rang and she saw the police chief's number, Callie groaned and forwarded the call to voicemail. Gale laughed.

"I take it they are still trying to win you guys back to their town?"

"Of course they are. She's tried everything from begging to threatening, but our lawyers have everything locked up. We are officially part of Brentwood, and I'm happy Grant Lake is finally on the map as a public destination."

"Well, you couldn't have made my father happier. Opening weekend was a huge success. The car show alone brought in close to twenty-thousand dollars for the local veterans association. I'm going to get out of your hair and let you get some sleep. See you tomorrow?"

"Absolutely," Callie said.

She followed Gale out to the porch and sat on the swing as she watched her leave. It was an utterly serene night. The water moved with a light wave from a cool fall breeze. Near the trees, Callie watched three figures emerge. The mother and daughter wore matching white gowns while the little boy ran around in a dapper gray suit. Callie smiled. It was the same clothes they'd been buried in.

The sight of Maria and her children dancing on the shore brought her comfort. She'd never spoken to them since the night of Frank and Collin's deaths. Something told her they would respond. Despite their presence there, the trio always seemed lost in their own world. It appeared to be one that offered joy far beyond what they found on earth.

"Momma?" Lizzy called out. "I had that nightmare again."

She jumped, her little girl appearing in the doorway. Lizzy rubbed her eyes before shuffling over to her mother and climbing into her lap. Slowly, Callie started to rock the swing back and forth as the figures dissipated into the air.

"Oh no! Is it the same one?"

Lizzy nodded.

"Awe, sweetheart, I'm sorry. Are you sure you don't want to tell me about it?"

She shrugged, much to Callie's surprise. Up until that point, she'd refused to tell Mike or Callie what it was that kept waking her at least once a week.

"Sometimes, it helps me if I talk through things. Even if I know they aren't real, it can still be scary."

It wasn't the time or place to tell Lizzy the truth about what had happened months ago. She was still too young to understand the power of the supernatural. Callie wasn't sure it was a story she would ever tell her daughter. Some things were simply better off left hidden in the closet with the rest of the Grant family skeletons.

For the most part, their time had passed with ease at the manor since the departure of the spirits. Still, late at night, Callie would find herself sleeping alone. She'd creep to the study door and find Mike hunched down over his grandfather's journals as if he were hunting for something, some shred of the reality that he had before.

"Daddy was being mean in the dream like he was when we first moved here and didn't know our friends were real."

Callie cringed. She remembered well how cold Mike had been. "That's not going to happen again, honey. We found homes for all our friends, and Daddy saw them right before they left."

"But what happens if Daddy becomes one of them, too? I don't want him to go away."

"Oh, my pet, your dad and I aren't going anywhere, I promise you."

"That's what you said in my dream, too," she grumbled. "Then you went away, Mommy, to live in the white dresses but not Daddy. Daddy stayed behind and got cranky like before."

"Shh, sweetheart. It was just a bad dream."

Callie shuddered, certain it was only the cool night air as she held Lizzy close. She closed her eyes and hummed the tune she'd learned in her dream. Everything was going to be okay. After all, kids had nightmares all the time. They never came true.

Printed in Great Britain
by Amazon

37760253R00169